Cover Copy

One soul bound mate...one quest to find her.

Year 1211, Scottish Highlands.

Duncan MacKenzie is the Laird of Ardan House, an honorable and fierce Highland warrior on the chase for a band of enemy warriors who are intent on his destruction, only as he hunts them down, he runs into a lass who poses the greatest challenge. He's drawn to the dark-haired enchantress who holds the fae ability to compel, a lass also intent on finding her brother who travels with the band of men he currently hunts. At every turn, she challenges his steely resolve, captivates and enthralls him, as well as unleashes his passion when it's never arisen for another woman before.

Spirited lass Ella Matheson is stunned to discover that the maddeningly rugged warrior hunting down her brother is the very man who makes her heart beat faster and her soul lift higher—a man who is her soul bound mate. Finding her chosen one within the enemy's ranks stuns her, yet she's never given up a challenge, and now she's bound and determined to bind this man who should be her enemy, right to her side.

Theirs is a battle of rivalry and dare, of untamed passion rising strong and true, and of a journey to forge the bond between two mates during a time of war.

Books by Joanne Wadsworth

The Matheson Brothers Series
Highlander's Desire, Book One
Highlander's Passion, Book Two
Highlander's Seduction, Book Three
Highlander's Kiss, Book Four
Highlander's Heart, Book Five
Highlander's Sword, Book Six
Highlander's Bride, Book Seven
Highlander's Caress, Book Eight
Highlander's Touch, Book Nine
Highlander's Shifter, Book Ten
Highlander's Claim, Book Eleven
Highlander's Courage, Book Twelve
Highlander's Mermaid, Book Thirteen

Highlander Heat Series
Highlander's Castle, Book One
Highlander's Magic, Book Two
Highlander's Charm, Book Three
Highlander's Guardian, Book Four
Highlander's Faerie, Book Five
Highlander's Champion, Book Six
Highlander's Captive (Short Story)

Billionaire Bodyguards Series
Billionaire Bodyguard Attraction, Book One
Billionaire Bodyguard Boss, Book Two
Billionaire Bodyguard Fling, Book Three

Books by Joanne Wadsworth

Regency Brides Series
The Duke's Bride, Book One
The Earl's Bride, Book Two
The Wartime Bride, Book Three
The Earl's Secret Bride, Book Four
The Prince's Bride, Book Five
Her Pirate Prince, Book Six

Princesses of Myth Series
Protector, Book One
Warrior, Book Two
Hunter (Short Story - Included in Warrior, Book Two)
Enchanter, Book Three
Healer, Book Four
Chaser, Book Five

Highlander's Caress

The Matheson Brothers, Book Eight

Joanne Wadsworth

Highlander's Caress
ISBN-13: 978-1-99-003438-1
Copyright © 2016, Joanne Wadsworth
Cover Art by Joanne Wadsworth
First electronic publication: June 2016

Joanne Wadsworth
http://www.joannewadsworth.com

AUTHOR'S NOTE:
This book is a work of fiction. The names, characters, places, and incidents are products of the writer's imagination or have been used fictitiously and are not to be construed as real. Any resemblance to persons, living or dead, actual events, locale or organizations is entirely coincidental. The author does not have any control over and does not assume any responsibility for third-party websites or their content.

Published in the United States of America

First digital publication: June 2016
First print publication: June 2016

The Fae Village

In the ninth century, the faerie king's youngest son visited a village along the shores of Loch Alsh and fell in love with the chief's daughter. The two wed and together created a half-blooded line born with the skills of the fae, a loyal line known as clan Matheson, a line guarded by the immortal fae princess, Cherub.

Duncan MacKenzie

The Isle of Skye, Scotland, 1211.

"Lower the sail. All to oars." In the dark of the night, Duncan MacKenzie stood at the helm of his war galley as his men saw to his orders. The sail swished down, and they slashed their oars into the deep waters of Loch Eishort, the wind rushing all around as they cruised ever closer toward Dunscaith Castle, the stronghold of his fiercest enemy.

A horn blasted across the bay, one loud and eerie peal, the point watchman clearly catching their arrival even under the blackness of the night sky. A second blast shrilled even louder and Duncan gritted his teeth. He'd tried to hide his arrival for as long as he could, but now the Chief of MacDonald would surely know his enemy approached, with absolute certainty.

At the stern, he fisted the hilt of his great two-handed claymore sitting snug at his side while up ahead, Dunscaith rose out of the dark, standing tall and strong on a low headland farther along the curve of the bay. The Fortress of Shadows 'twas called. An apt name, the castle always hidden within the murky shadows of the night each time he'd visited. Even now, only the merest touch of candlelight flickered ghostlike from the tower windows, the hefty swell of the sea surging in and battering the cliff-face rising high all around the heavily fortified keep.

With the stronghold built on an off-shore rock connected to the Isle of Skye by a walled bridge that spanned a gap of twenty feet or so, this fortress was near impenetrable. Only a sliver of pebbly sand sat to one side where the sea-gate butted into the stronghold, the guardsmen patrolling the battlements high above able to see with a bird's eye view out across the bay and along Skye's coastline to the west.

At the bow, his squire sat with wide eyes on the dreaded keep, the white flag he'd handed the lad when they'd set out earlier this night clenched tight in his fist.

Their time had arrived. He strode up the aisle and halted as he came abreast of Hamish standing at the center mast. Around him, his men continued to power through the rolling waves, their breath heaving and strength immense as they sent their galley cruising swiftly toward their destination. No hesitation. He had none either.

"I dinnae *see* this trip ending well." Hamish, his second-in-command, eyed him, his man one of the full-blooded fae who held "the sight." Hamish received visions whenever harm was about to befall them, had been instrumental in ensuring all had gone well for Duncan and his men of late.

"My father has been at war with the MacDonald for far too long, as have I. 'Tis time to lay our disputes to rest."

"The MacDonald has no desire for peace talks. He wants to rule these isles and all within them."

"A marriage of alliance could end our warring." His father had put the proposal toward him, asked him to take it to the MacDonald.

"You too hold fae blood." Hamish lowered his voice, his words traveling no farther than him. "One day you might discover you're mated, and then there will be naught you can do about claiming the lass if you've gone and wed yourself to another."

"I would have sensed the bond taking form afore now if I were in fact mated." He kept his voice low as well. On board none knew of his fae blood which had come to him through his mother's Matheson line, a mother he'd never known, would never know.

"That isnae always the way of the bond. We can only sense our chosen one once we've met them."

"Then I'd have to set foot on Matheson land for that to occur, which I've only done once in all my years." With one hand raised, he motioned to his squire and gave him the signal to wave the white flag.

At the edge of the sea-gate, a guardsman caught the fluttering cloth on the long stick as the lad thrust it from side to side. The guard hailed a warning shout to the sentry on the winding stairs, the man echoing the shout to the head guardsman on the ramparts above.

"Our time has come." Duncan drew in a long, fortifying breath. "Let's see if we can make it past their welcoming party."

"I'll be right beside you every step of the way."

"Aye, as you've always been." From the bow, he cupped his hands to his mouth and called to the MacDonald warriors standing at the sea-gate, "I am Duncan MacKenzie, the Laird of Ardan House, second-born son of Colin MacKenzie and I've come to speak to the Chief of MacDonald. I wish to enter into peace talks with him this night."

Into the water, four of the MacDonald's men waded toward him then gripped the sides of his vessel, their swords and battle axes hooked at their sides. The head man's drilling gaze landed on him, a gory red scar crossing his forehead, one that barely missed his eye as it flowed down one cheek. "Ye'll need to await confirmation from my chief afore being permitted any farther onto our land."

"Duncan MacKenzie!" The Chief of MacDonald thundered down the winding stairs in his great plaid, his massive claymore holstered to his back, the hilt bobbing and catching the moonlight now peppering through the thick layer of darkened cloud above. The man's beady black eyes glinted in the yellow torchlight at the base of the stony landing. "You're fortunate I have no' yet told my archers to release their arrows. By what means have you sailed to my shores this night with your flag of parley raised?"

"I've come at my father's request. Colin MacKenzie wishes for a reconciliation between our clans." Over the edge of the galley, he bounded and splashed into the water. He'd come and now would do his best to secure this proposal. Surging through the waves, he cut a fast path toward his enemy, gripped the stone landing and hoisted himself up. Water sluiced to his booted feet, his black battle leathers slick and wet, his weapons strapped to his body in every conceivable place. He might have accepted his father's challenge to sail to Dunscaith for peace talks, but that didn't mean he wouldn't protect and defend himself if the need arose. "I ask for you to hear me out this night."

"There will be no peace talks between us." MacDonald glared at Duncan's men who rose to their feet in the galley at his snarl. "If either you or any of your men attempt to take my stronghold, I'll ensure you're all slaughtered where you stand."

"Remain at ease." He stilled his warriors with one hand then to the MacDonald muttered, "My chief requests a marriage of alliance between our clans, and I hereby ask for a formal betrothal agreement to be made between your eldest daughter and myself. 'Tis time to mend the discord between our clans and to move forward. What do you say?"

"Discord? You call our feud that of a simple discord?" Hands fisted at his sides and the muscle in his jaw ticking, MacDonald seethed with anger. "Naught but decades of warring and bloodshed lie between our clans and I will never, ever shackle my eldest daughter to you."

"I would treasure her, ensure she remained well cared for and of course free to visit you as often as either you or she wished." His mission to end this warring and gain a betrothal agreement was too important to walk away from now. "I give you my word that would be so."

"Your word?" The MacDonald spat at his feet. "That is what I think of your—"

"Chief!" A MacDonald guardsman shouted as he ran along the barbican, one hand waving toward the tip of the bay. "Another MacKenzie galley approaches."

Duncan jerked around. Hell and damnation. His father's double-mast galley skimmed the waves toward him, his men slashing their oars through the tumbling waves. At the bow, a marksman stood with his longbow and sent an arrow soaring. It arched high then swished down and *thunked* into the ground, right between him and the MacDonald.

Scowling, MacDonald hauled the arrow from between the cracks in the rocky landing, gripped both ends and snapped it in half over one raised knee. He bellowed to his men on the battlements, "Archers, move into position." A score of warriors raised longbows and slotted their arrows into place. "Release the arrows. Dinnae allow Colin MacKenzie near our shores."

Flying high, arrows whizzed over Duncan's head, one after the other before slicing down and pinging off shields his father's warriors shoved high over their heads. A roar boomed from his father's men and the galley caught a peaking wave and glided the whitecaps into shore. As the hull scraped the sea floor, his father and his men bounded over the side and swarmed onto the thin strip of the pebbly shoreline. With a fist pumped into the air, his father released a blood-curdling battle cry. "We take Dunscaith!"

"You are as devious as your father." MacDonald snarled and snapped at Duncan, thrust his sword high and swung.

Duncan whipped his claymore free and met the deadly blow. Damn his scheming father. He'd placed all their lives on the line this night with his deceitful ways. "I was unaware of my father's intent to join us."

The MacDonald's warriors thundered down the sea-gate stairs and Duncan's men, left with no choice, bounded from his vessel and flooded the beach. The two clans crashed together with a mighty boom, steel ringing loud against steel.

"Your blood and that of every MacKenzie warrior who attacks my clan will soon soak this soil." Gaze venomous, the MacDonald swung.

Elbows locked tight, Duncan caught the blow a mere inch from his nose, shoved one foot back and held his position while all around him within the near dark, his warriors fought on. Swords sliced into limbs and blood splattered the ground from both clans. Red swirled within the water and muddied the wash spilling onto the shore and across the slick landing.

"Gavin!" The MacDonald yelled to his nephew who hoisted from the water onto the stone landing behind Duncan. He'd met Gavin on the battlefield before and the warrior was a sly devil, devious and scheming.

Digging his feet in, Duncan met first Gavin's blow then the MacDonald's, both well-timed strikes following hard on the heels of the other as they kept him pinned between them.

"I'll enjoy ridding these isles of you." Gavin snorted, his red hair lying slick to his scalp and his beady black eyes glinting.

"I'm here." Hamish heaved out of the water onto the landing next to him and slammed his blade into the MacDonald who caught his strike.

"All here will halt their fighting and listen to me well and true!" A piercing shout broke the battle and halted Duncan's sword arm. "Every warrior with a weapon will lower it." High on the battlements, a woman wearing tan pants and a vest over a white shirt stood at the corner crenellation, her dark locks streaming behind her in the wind and her voice rising strong and true. "Those from clan MacKenzie will retreat, and those from clan MacDonald will allow them to leave."

Her fiercely compelling voice smothered him, drew him deep within her demand. Both the MacDonald and Gavin lowered their swords.

"You have a Matheson compeller in your midst?" Father snapped from along the beach. He scowled as he jerked backward through the swell, the lass's demand that they retreat forcing his father back toward his galley.

"Aye, and your fight this night is done, Colin MacKenzie." The lass glared at his father. "I am Ella from the House of Clan Matheson, and you will obey every word I speak. Gather your fallen and leave these shores."

Father's warriors slung their fallen comrades over their shoulders and stumbled through the waves and boarded their vessel. Duncan's own men did the same, returning their injured to his galley.

"Be gone!" Ella's hypnotic voice rang even louder, the gold flecks in her brown eyes flickering as she moved her gaze to him. "You too, Duncan MacKenzie. Leave, and know that my Matheson kinsmen are allied with clan MacDonald. Never will we allow you to take Dunscaith."

So captivating. This spellbinding woman radiated such strength and passion. "You have done me the greatest favor this night." He dipped his head in acknowledgement, lifted it again.

"Aye, I have. I've saved your big hide, so make sure once you leave, you dinnae return." She leaned over the crenellation. "No more shall you fight this night. Am I understood?"

"I didnae wish for this battle, and never would I raise arms against you or any of your Matheson kin." Not when he too held Matheson fae blood.

"I would win any battle if you did." A teasing smile suddenly lifted her lips and she winked at him, actually winked.

Naught more could have caught him off-guard.

"I would like to see you again."

"Please, dinnae think to toy and flirt with me." Frowning, she motioned to his vessel and issued one more command he could no longer ignore. "I said leave."

"Come." Hamish dragged at his arm.

Aye, he'd leave since he'd surely outstayed his welcome now. He jumped off the landing and splashed to his galley then along with his men, boarded his vessel.

Out of the bay, they rowed then raised the sail and caught the fresh breeze, the intriguing lass becoming naught more than a mere dot on the ramparts.

As he lost complete sight of her, his chest ached and a deep need to return to her slashed through him. Well, it appeared Ella Matheson wasn't only a compeller, but an enchantress who could steal a man's reason as well. "One day," he murmured under his breath, "I will find you Ella Matheson and when I do, I intend to learn all I can about you."

Aye, he wouldn't rest until he'd spoken to her once more. Unraveling all her secrets would surely be a delight.

Cherub – The Fae Princess and Guardian to her Earthbound Kind

On the cliffs near Loch Carron, Scotland, a month later.

Under an endless array of twinkling stars and a gloriously heavy moon, Cherub stood unseen on the cliffs as the ocean swelled with white-tipped waves that glowed a silvery-gold in the moonlight below. Kirk, her soul bound mate, towered over her from behind, his big body a heavenly wall of heat as her cloaking remained extended over them both. "Ella Matheson sails this way with her brother." She rested back fully against him. "Directly toward Duncan MacKenzie."

"You believe these two truly are soul bound?"

"Aye, although their mated bond will be a difficult match to make with their clans so at war." The wind rushed all around, fluttering her white fur cloak about her legs and lifting her blond hair and snagging it within Kirk's bristles. Something within the rising wind also tickled further at her fae senses and arms raised, she allowed the *air*, the element she controlled, to bring to her each and every secret it held. "They'll meet at the tavern this night."

"Might we watch that meeting?" Kirk nuzzled her neck and she tipped her head to the side to give him greater access.

"We might be too busy." She moaned as he nipped her flesh.

"In what way?" He tugged the shoulder of her gown lower, slid one hand beneath the soft velvet and cupped her breast.

"I believe you know in what way." Heat rippled through her and her need for even more of his delicious touch flared strong. "Duncan is Ella's match in every way, just as you are mine."

"Will we be guiding them in the days to come?"

"Aye, as is needed, but we'll remain hidden for most of the time."

"I love remaining hidden with you." Kirk scooped her up, strode to the lush grass behind them and lowered her to the ground.

"As I love remaining hidden with you, my temping bear." With one hand on his chest, the other curled around his nape and the sweetly sensual night breeze washing over her, she gave herself over to her chosen one.

"I want to feel your skin against mine."

"I want that too."

He leaned in and kissed her, every wickedly muscled inch of his body pressed hard against hers and together, they got lost in their love, their bodies and souls entwined as one and their need for each other an unstoppable beat that neither could ever deny.

This was love. The soul bond.

This was what she wanted for each and every one of her fae blooded kind.

This was what she would deliver.

Chapter 1
First Encounters Are Never Forgotten

Nearing the entrance to Loch Carron, an hour later.

The foamy tips of the rolling waves glistened gold in the moonlight as Ella Matheson sailed her skiff with her brother. "'Tis quiet out on the water this night."

"Unusually so." Ethan scanned the rugged shoreline with its high cliffs and forested hills. "'Tis almost like the calm before the storm."

"Well, we are nearing MacKenzie land, so we should expect a storm sooner or later." Usually of the battling sort. She turned the rudder a touch. Ethan had been with her that night on Dunscaith's battlements a month past when Duncan MacKenzie and his devious father had attempted to take the MacDonald's stronghold.

"You still dinnae have an answer do you?" Lifting one curious brow, Ethan eyed her.

"Do you mean about Duncan?"

"Aye, it took you telling him twice to leave afore he did. Never have I seen a man no' jump immediately to do your hypnotic bidding. His relief at hearing your compelling command was also clear to see. I dinnae believe he had any knowledge of his father's plan to attack, his surprise at Colin's arrival the same as the MacDonald's."

"Death would surely have been his if I'd no' intervened." The MacKenzies had been well outnumbered. Why they'd even thought to attack with so few men had confused her at first, made her hesitate before she'd issued her compelling commands.

"Aye, and now we sail directly toward his land. Let's pray we dinnae run into him this night." Hand to his brow, Ethan peered toward the thick line of the woods edging the high cliffs where the forest rose sure and strong, the tall pines swaying in the brisk ocean breeze.

Only a mile or two away Duncan's stronghold sat, although Ardan House wasn't hers or Ethan's intended destination and never would be. Aye, they sailed to the tavern belonging to William and Mary, the only two MacKenzie allies they'd ever have in this war between their clans.

"There is naught more I love than sailing these seas." Ethan dipped one hand over the side of the skiff and skimmed the waves with his fingers. The wind rose and whipped his dark mop of curly locks all about. A warrior he was, as tall and strong as Papa had ever been.

"Aye, for me too." She breathed deep of the salty sea air. Up above, the moon snuck behind a shadowy cloud while toward the tavern, a thick curl of smoke drifted into the night sky.

Over the swell, she guided their boat toward the stone landing and as they cruised in, Ethan lowered the sail then nabbed the oars and rowed the last few feet. They bumped gently against the landing and Ethan uncoiled the mooring rope, bounded out and secured their skiff to its mooring.

"Pass me the bags." Ethan held out his hands for them, his

heavy black coat swishing about his legs and the sharp length of his sword glinting inside the draping folds.

She wriggled the bags out from under the seat where she'd stowed them. Bulky yet fairly light since they were filled with naught but wool, she lobbed first one sack to him and then the other before jumping onto the landing beside him. Taking care, she snuck a glance across the other side of the sea-gate where a war galley bobbed with two guardsmen keeping a watch from the bow. At the top of the center mast, a flag rippled in the breeze, one displaying the MacKenzie clan crest upon it.

"Keep your head down," Ethan whispered in her ear.

"They are harmless enough to you and I considering our skills."

"Still, we'll take all care." He slung the bags over his shoulders and motioned for her to go first along the landing.

Patting her woolen cap to make certain not even one errant lock of her long hair had escaped, she walked toward the beach then up the grassy rise in her black breeches and riding boots that laced all the way to her knees. On the higher land overlooking the ocean, the tavern sat with the forest rising sure behind it.

Uphill, she trekked and as she reached the gravelly courtyard, she halted as a squeal rang out from somewhere nearer the far trees. The moon highlighted the outline of a warrior standing under the canopy of a wide elm, his hand curved around the hip of a maid in a green kirtle. He groped her breasts, while another warrior leaning against the wall of the stables twenty feet away, hooted his encouragement.

Naught infuriated her more than seeing a lass being so terribly manhandled. She stormed toward them, determined to compel the warrior to leave the maid be and take his own cock in hand if he wished for some relief, only the lass giggled and rocked her hips against the warrior's.

Ethan caught her arm, shook his head. "She wishes for his attention, Ella."

The lass moaned as the warrior freed himself and hoisted her skirts.

Unfortunately, she'd stumbled across her fair share of warriors taking maids wherever they pleased. Either in a darkened niche in their chief's castle, the stables, or some other such place. Ethan was right.

"Come." Ethan nudged her toward the tavern. "We have bags to deliver."

"Dinnae you ever tup a lass like that." She snorted under her breath. "You'll wait for your chosen one, just as I have and continue to do."

"One day you'll find him." A sure look crossed his face.

"Aye, and when I do I'll blast him for making me wait so long."

"That I long to see." Grinning, he looped one arm around her shoulders and steered her under the curved overhang of the tavern's front door.

On the rushes at the entrance, she stamped the dirt from her booted feet, opened the large paneled door and walked inside. Along with a rush of warmth from the roaring fire came the riotous babble of voices which always infused this tavern. Within the main room warriors, farmers, and travelers aplenty enjoyed bread and stew as they chatted, each table separated from the other by wooden screens which allowed a touch of privacy.

"I'll take these bags through to William. Stay out of trouble while I'm gone." Ethan tweaked her nose.

"I always stay out of trouble."

"Ha, of course you do." Chuckling, he strode down the corridor leading toward William's solar where he could always be found if he was not in the main room conversing with his patrons. William might be a MacKenzie, but he was also loyal to clan Matheson, his mother having been of fae blood. Mary, his wife, had been from their fae village and one of her mama's dearest friends.

Mary swished around the tables in her blue gown, her lacy shawl slipping from one shoulder as she poured ale into tankards. Ella raised a hand and waved out.

Surprise lit Mary's face as she caught sight of her. She set her jug down, hurried across and smothered her in a fierce hug. "'Tis so good to see you. Hannah didnae come with you?" She peered toward the front door.

"Nay, no' this time. Mama has no' been feeling her best, but she's weaved a great deal of wool this month and Ethan and I have brought two bags full for you to take to the market. Ethan's already gone on ahead to give it to William."

"William has the coin from the last sale. We fetched a fair price." Mary squeezed her cheeks. "Look at you all dressed as a lad again. When will I ever see you in a gown? I cannae remember the last time."

"'Tis far easier to sail the seas this way, as well as remain unnoticed while I do."

"Well, that is true and I wouldnae want you to take any undue risks, no' that William or I would ever allow any harm to come to you here. Oh," she babbled in a rush, "we also must speak of an important matter." She lowered her voice and pulled her back into the darkened niche under the stairwell. "Word is a fae compeller halted the recent attack by Colin MacKenzie at Dunscaith. I take it that was you?"

"Aye, 'twas me."

"I was pleased to hear of it, that you'd halted the feud from becoming far worse." Mary nodded. "Although what Colin MacKenzie was thinking by sailing in after Duncan and causing such a raucous, I'll never know. He had asked his son to enter into a betrothal agreement with the MacDonald's eldest daughter and that was what Duncan intended on doing."

"Duncan never knew of his father's ploy?"

"Nay, and our laird has no' spoken to his father since that

night."

"Do you know the laird well?"

"Duncan's here, right above-stairs meeting with some of his men in one of our private rooms. Even though you halted the battle at Dunscaith, he's still been under attack from the MacDonald's nephew in the weeks since. Gavin sneaks onto Duncan's land, has slaughtered his cattle, a fair number of head." Mary knotted her lacy shawl at the front. "Duncan hunts him, intends on teaching the man a lesson."

"I had no' heard of Gavin's attacks."

"Aye, he's a menace that man is."

A menace clearly she and Ethan needed to find and speak to, or more importantly, compel. If there was something she could do to ease the tensions between the clans, then she'd do it. "Leave this with me, Mary. I'll see what I can do to aid you all."

"'Twould be much appreciated."

Footsteps pounded from above them and a dozen warriors wearing the MacKenzie tartan and heavy weaponry marched downstairs and entered the main room. At the head of the group strode Duncan himself. She'd never mistake him. He stood a good two hands over six feet, his massive two-handed claymore bobbing in the baldric strapped across his broad back. With his great plaid hooked around his waist and looped over one shoulder, he appeared every inch the mighty warrior she'd witnessed fighting in battle.

"I must go and see to the laird and his men. Stay here until I return." Mary tucked a loose red lock from her top-knot behind her ear, snuck out and joined the men. She led them across the room to the tables underneath the far window, although Duncan remained standing at the base of the stairs, unmoving.

Muscles rippled as he rolled his shoulders, then as he turned, the light from the fire caught the dark stubble grazing his jaw and lit it a heavenly blue hue, the ends of his short black locks as well.

"Who goes there?" He peered into the darkened recess where she remained.

Oh goodness. She hardly needed to come face to face with him again, and certainly not here on his soil. Carefully, slowly, she backed away then ducked down the passageway and snuck inside the closest door and shut it behind herself.

Leaning back against the grooved wood, she let out a relieved breath and surveyed the antechamber. This private room with its lit fire and large central table surrounded by six high-backed chairs often housed men as they enjoyed a game or two of cards after a meal, but thankfully right now it remained perfectly clear.

She pushed off the door and walked past two burgundy padded armchairs in the corner next to William's treasured chess set sitting on a low table between the two chairs. A flask of wine and two silver goblets sat next to the board with its wooden chess pieces, all lined up for a game. Mayhap someone had requested the room. If they had, she couldn't remain here for too long.

The door whooshed open and Duncan filled the entrance, his brilliant blue gaze narrowing in on her. "Well, well, it appears you wish to hide from me, lad. Whatever for?"

Drat. It appeared there would be no steering clear of Duncan this night. She crossed her arms with a slap and muttered, "I'm no' a lad, but the very lass who saved your big hide last month."

His gaze flickered with surprise as he skimmed her from head to toe. "The only lass to save my supposedly big hide of late, happened to be a compeller by the name of Ella Matheson." Small wrinkles fanned out from his expressive eyes as he studied her. "Remove your cap."

"I'll do no such thing."

"Do you fear me?"

"Hardly." She always stood her ground, no matter her

position.

"So I noticed during our battle on Skye. You're also the very lass I'd hoped to find one day and express my gratitude to, although I never considered I might encounter you right here on my land. Would it be Mary you're here to see? She was a Matheson afore she wed William, and even William's mother holds a touch of fae blood." His drilling gaze intensified. "Are you close kin at all?"

"Mary and my mama are friends. William and Mary are both kin and always will be."

"Interesting." He closed the door with a soft click and slid the bolt home. "I've a great desire to know more about you, Ella Matheson, and it appears I've only just scraped the surface."

"Then you'd better first learn that I cannae be intimidated." She tipped her head toward the bolted door. "That bolt willnae keep me from leaving should I wish to."

"I didnae lock the door to keep you contained, only to keep anyone else from entering while we speak." He cocked a brow. "You scuttled in here so fast I barely caught the sight of you fleeing."

"I didnae flee."

"Of course you did." He stepped closer, almost towering over her. "That made the chase even more intriguing though."

"I simply wished for a moment of privacy." The man exuded power from every inch of his tall form, although with only one uttered word she could bring him to his knees if she so desired. "What is it you wish to speak to me about?"

"Your powerful skill and how you used it to ensure the battle came to a swift end." He uncrossed his arms and gestured to one of the armchairs. "Sit, please. I truly mean you no harm. I owe you my life, will forever be in your debt." He sank down into one of the armchairs and picked up the wine flask. "It appears we have refreshments. Do you care to join me for a drink?"

This man intrigued her, and far more than any other man ever had. She eased into the chair opposite him and motioned for him to pour.

"Thank you. I see you prefer lad's clothing, Ella, if I might call you Ella? I certainly do apologize for mistaking you for a lad just now." He poured ruby-red wine into both goblets, held one out to her and lowered his tone to a suddenly husky level, "Such attire suits you, if I might say so."

"You're flirting with me again, as you did at Dunscaith."

"I'm simply stating a fact, although should you wish to believe I'm currently flirting, so be it."

"You're a wretched man, Duncan, that's if I might call you Duncan?" She accepted the wine from him and took a hearty sip.

"Of course. First names it is then." He sipped his wine, tapped his leg. "I never intended for things to escalate at Dunscaith as they did, only my father made that nigh on impossible with his unexpected arrival."

"Mary said you wished to enter into a betrothal agreement."

"Aye, although that's now no longer possible." He leaned forward, elbows braced to his knees and his goblet held securely between both hands. "Sitting here with you is something I never imagined possible. Do you travel alone often?"

"I'm here with my brother. Ethan and I had business to attend to with William and Mary."

"Have you sailed from your fae village or Dunscaith Castle?" He took a hearty swallow of his wine then chased a bead of red at the corner of his mouth with his tongue.

Oh my, he had such deliciously full lips. Not that she should be noticing his lips.

"Ella?" One raised brow.

"Pardon?"

"I asked if you'd sailed from your fae village or Dunscaith Castle?"

"I only visit Dunscaith from time to time. Ethan and I live

with our mama at the village." She cleared her throat. "Mary informed me of Gavin MacDonald's attacks when I arrived. 'Tis the first of heard of him slaughtering your cattle, but you can be assured I'll do whatever I can to halt him. Ethan too. My brother and I always act as one in our desire to seek peace."

"There will never be any peace between Gavin and I." He set his wine down, straightened the chess board and righted one or two of the misaligned pieces. "Do you play the King's Game?"

"My papa taught me how to play after returning with our chief from visiting the king at Stirling Castle. He made this very board for William and carved these chess pieces as well. He whittled them from wood Ethan and I collected in the woods."

"I had no idea. I've always admired this set. 'Tis well crafted, with great attention to detail." He picked up another piece and rubbed it between his thumb and forefinger before gently setting it back down. "My foster sister, Kyla, loves naught more than besting me in this game. She says it requires a man or woman to consider multiple strategies when making a move, which is true, much as one must do when coming up against a fierce opponent on the battlefield. Do you care to play with me?"

"Playing with you could be dangerous." Although unable to help herself, she shuffled forward in her seat. Making the first move, she selected a piece and slid it across the board and into position. Aye, naught more did she thrive on than coming up against a new opponent, and Duncan MacKenzie made one very fine one at that.

"Yet you're a fae compeller, while I'm merely a warrior with the ability to wield a blade. It should be me who says playing with you could be dangerous." He moved his chosen piece, the fire's glow flickering across his high cheeks.

"Aye, with one word I could alter this game."

"You would cheat against me?" Moving swiftly, he reached across, nabbed her woolen cap from her head and dropped it into her lap before easing back and eyeing her long locks as they swished down and swayed about her waist. "My apologies, but I needed to see more of you."

"I'll certainly cheat if you do that again." He had the reflexes of a warrior, swift and precise and she'd best not forget it. She wound her hair back up and stuffed her cap overtop of it, tugged the wool down good and proper so he couldn't so easily do that again. "So, would you truly have wed the MacDonald's daughter to end this current feud?"

"Aye, do you no' agree a marriage of alliance would have been worthwhile?"

"Such marriages arenae the way of my clan. We wait for our chosen one to claim us then join only with them."

"I'm aware of how your people join together when mated." He searched her gaze. "Are you wed, Ella, or do you still await your chosen one?"

"I wait, as patiently as I can."

"What if he never comes?"

"He will."

"You have such faith." Gently, he laid his hand over top of hers and whispered, "Turn your hand over."

For some reason she did, until their palms lay flush together and a new warmth enveloped her and rippled outward from her core.

With the softest caress, he stroked her palm with his thumb in one very slow, enticing circle, his gaze holding hers and not wavering one bit. "You, Ella, are the most intriguing lass I've ever met."

* * * *

Ella's decree that she awaited her chosen one continued to echo through Duncan's mind, his need to touch her stirring him deep within. He'd asked her to turn her hand over and she had, and now he wanted even more, to eliminate the distance between them and extinguish this separation.

Aye, from the moment he'd walked into this antechamber, she'd stunned him, caught him in some silken web of desire until all he could focus on was her. Such sooty lashes framed her beautiful brown eyes with their intriguing flecks of gold. When he'd snatched her cap, her lush hair had unraveled in a mass of rich brown blended with streaks of shimmering gold. Hell, he could drown in her stunning gaze, wanted only to lose himself in it. "You've bewitched me, Ella Matheson."

"I can assure you I've done naught of the kind." She tugged her hand free of his and with slightly shaky fingers gripped her goblet and sipped her wine, even splashed some over the rim as she set it jerkily back down.

"Mayhap even more than bewitched." A piper's merry tune echoed in from under the door, the entertainment in the main room having begun. He stood, caught her hand again and pulled her to her feet. "Would you care for a birl?"

"We were playing a game."

"And now I wish to dance."

"I think no'."

"There's no need to fear my touch."

"I fear naught." She stepped toe to toe with him, pressed one hand against his chest and with a tilt to her head, swirled one finger down over his abs and along the waistband of his belted kilt. "See, no fear at all."

"You play with fire, my grumpy one." He wrapped one arm around her waist, pulled her closer and rocked from foot to foot. All he wished to do was feel her sliding sensuously against him, those black breeches of hers hugging every mouthwatering curve.

"This isnae a dance I've ever indulged in afore."

"Neither have I. How often do you come to this tavern?"

"On the first of each month."

"I've no wish to wait that long afore I see you again." He dipped her backward, leaned over her and rubbed his cheek against her cheek. "You feel so good in my arms."

"Oh goodness, what are you doing?" Her breath whooshed from her and she grasped ahold of his shoulders, her cap falling off and her luscious locks sweeping down to the floor.

The firelight flickered across her face in shimmering shades of red and gold and he became far more than bewitched.

"It might be best if you release me. Should my brother walk in and see us like this, I dinnae know what he will do. Likely attack you. He holds the battle skill and can be rather overprotective of me."

"I bolted the door. Meet me somewhere, anywhere. I must see you again afore the first of the next month. Name the place and time and I will be there."

"There can only ever be danger should we meet again. Let me go." She looked deep into his eyes. "Release me."

Her hypnotic demand clouded his thoughts and she said something else as he set her back on her feet. Something about listen well and pay attention. Her next words though rang with strong intensity, flooding his mind.

"From this moment forth, you'll consider me naught more than an annoyance, and one you never wish to lay eyes upon again. Do you understand me, Duncan?"

"Aye, I understand." His head spun, her powerfully spoken command one he couldn't ignore.

"Repeat what I said."

"You're naught more than an annoyance to me, and one I never wish to lay eyes upon again."

"That's perfect." With a soft smile, she lifted up on her toes and murmured in his ear, "Close your eyes and count to one-hundred, nice and slow. Once you're done, you may open your eyes again and when you do, you'll find me gone from this place and you'll be most glad I've left."

"Aye, one-hundred and I'll be glad to see you gone." Yet deep inside his heart, it screamed out a denial. Still, he closed his eyes and did as she'd bid. 'Twas impossible to deny her hypnotic request. "One, two, three…"

Slowly, her fingers slipped free of his and his heart heaved.

Pain slashed through him. Damn her ability to compel.

The door shut with a soft snick.

Chapter 2

Sailing along the Sound of Raasay, near MacKenzie land, two weeks later.

Sailing through the choppy waters, Duncan continued his search for the Chief of MacDonald's nephew. Gavin and his band of men had been slaughtering his cattle for weeks, sneaking onto his land and causing sheer mayhem and now he'd had more than enough. He needed to catch up with the man and halt him in his tracks, and preferably by ensuring his death.

With the ropes in hand, he searched the shoreline as the blustery wind filled his galley's sail. "All eyes alert," he bellowed to his men. "We're closing in on our prey. I can sense it."

"Do you smell that, Duncan?" Hamish, his second, kept a lookout from the bow.

Nose to the air, he drew in the salty scent of the sea. It enveloped his senses, and there, a hint of smoke wafted on the breeze. "A fire rages."

"We're almost at Inverarish." Hamish's dark hair whipped about in the wind, the skies darkening as night drew nearer.

"Gavin knows the village of Inverarish falls under my

protection." He wrestled with the ropes, turned the sail a touch and caught more wind as the sun dipped along the horizon and sent a final streak of brilliant red through the haze of dark blue. "We sail to the village, with all haste."

They rounded the tip, the waves churning and the scent of the smoke thickening. Along the stony shoreline of the bay, flames licked a fiery orange-red across the thatched-roof of a longhouse. Smoke billowed from doors and windows and embers whistled through the wind and snatched ahold of the next rooftop. Villagers swarmed from the houses with wooden pails in hand and herded down toward the water's edge. In a living line of men, women, and children, they dipped pails into the surf and swung them from one hand to the next.

"All to oars," he bellowed and dropped the sail. Another house caught alight and more ashy smoke plumed into the night sky and smothered the bay. To the bow, he bounded and as they crested the waves twenty feet from the shoreline, he leapt over the side and splashed through the hip-deep water toward the villagers. Shoving forward, he slogged in then jogged to the head of the line where James, the stocky inn owner, yelled orders.

"You've good timing, my laird." James jabbed a finger toward the forest rising high along the upper rim of the bay overlooking the village. "Gavin MacDonald and his band of men snuck in from the forest and attacked, have filched several horses from our stables and now fled the same way they came. The lass made chase."

"Which lass?" The winds fanned the flames. He hollered to his men as they spilled from the vessel onto the shore, "The fires must be put out! Aid wherever you can."

"The lass Ella Matheson. Her brother, Ethan, was with Gavin and his men and she's been searching for Ethan and arrived here naught more than an hour ago." James heaved a pail forward along the line. "She said Ethan has successfully infiltrated Gavin's band of men and attempts to halt Gavin's devious behavior from within it."

"She's a compeller and her clan is allied with the MacDonald's." She was also a terrible annoyance, a lass he never wished to see again, and that thought rang like a death knell through his head, had since that night they'd met at William's tavern.

"Ella took a chest illness a sennight ago, isnae fully recovered yet. Her voice is raspy, her ability to compel coming and going." James aided a woman carrying a bairn—her face blackened by the grimy smoke—into the spot behind him then lifted the cubby-faced child from her shoulders and hefted the wee lad onto his own. "Ethan is much like his father, Ella too," James continued. "All here remember Hacon Matheson and how he fought for the rights of all, no matter which clan they belonged to. Ella and Ethan do all they can to honor their father's memory. Peace is what they desire, no' war."

"James is right. Ella and Ethan always fight to make things right." Hamish gripped his shoulder, his gaze firm on his. "A vision just assailed me and I've *seen* you should go and aid her. I'll take care of one and all here."

The last thing he wanted to do was leave these villagers when every hand was needed to douse the fires, yet Hamish had never set him on the wrong path before and if he said he needed to go, then he would go. "This village is under my care. Gavin's hit here is a direct strike against me and 'tis unacceptable." He wouldn't tolerate such treacherous attacks. "Hamish, ensure no lives are lost this night. I'll return as soon as I can."

"I shall, and watch out for the low branch as you ride." Hamish heaved a pail forward. "Go easy on the lass too. You've expressed a sudden dislike of her these past few weeks, and that worries me."

"She frustrates me, more than any other lass ever has." Although, no more could he delay if he wished to catch up to her. He sprinted up the beach and raced across the grassy verge, bounded over the top beam of the corral and snagged a horse, the animal thankfully already saddled. "Open the gate," he hollered to the lanky stable hand.

"If ye are after Mistress Ella, she took the entrance to the forest at the top of the hill, followed in the tracks of the MacDonalds and her brother." In loose breeches and a dirt-smeared tunic, the lad swung the gate wide and pointed to the place he spoke of.

"You have my thanks." Knees shoved into the horse's flanks, he burst out of the stables and rode along the winding upward trail that rimmed the village. As the skies darkened further, he plunged into the depths of the forest and followed the tracks heading to the east.

* * * *

In the near dark, Ella bolted along the forest trail, her horse snorting frosty air and the wind plastering her tunic to her chest and breeches to her legs. Fallen leaves and pine needles twirled as she urged her horse to a faster pace and hurtled on. She had to catch up to Ethan, to do all she could to aid him in halting Gavin in his tracks. She also intended on blasting her brother for leaving her behind at their village on the mainland, no matter that she'd been ill. Thankfully, he'd successfully infiltrated Gavin's band of men. At least that she could be grateful for. Ensuring peace was now within their grasp.

The wind rushed all around, swept her woolen cap from her head and sent it smacking into the wide trunk of an oak tree behind her. Blast it. That was her favorite cap. No time to retrieve that. Head down, she hugged her steed tighter as she followed the scored tracks in the trail sprinkled with moonlight penetrating through the thick canopy overhead.

Up ahead, the pounding of horses' hooves ricocheted toward her. She was close, and gaining on them. When she caught up with Gavin she intended on halting his madness once and for all. No more stealing and slaughtering cattle, no more setting fires and burning down the homes of innocent villagers, and certainly no more vindictive attacks against Duncan MacKenzie. If he wanted to raise the stakes in the battle between their clans, he was doing a very prime job of it.

"Ella!"

She swung a look over her shoulder. Drat. 'Twas Duncan himself. In battle leathers and his claymore bobbing in a baldric across his back, his blue eyes blazed as he charged in beside her. "What are you doing here?" Her raspy voice barely made a noise.

"James said your voice comes and goes and he's clearly right. I'll hunt down Gavin and his men, bring your brother back as well. Head back to the village. There's no need for you to be out in the cold this night, not when you're still recovering from whatever illness you've had."

"You dinnae command me." Ethan was her brother. She'd be the one to find him.

"I said head back." He rushed ahead and dust swirled in her face. "Return, now," he bellowed over his shoulder.

"'Tis you who should head back." Not that he would have caught her whispered comeback. Aye, never would she abandon her brother when he needed her so greatly. She snapped her horse's reins and picked up her pace, rode up alongside Duncan and shot him a fierce look, wished only her voice could be just as fierce too. "Be gone with you."

"You cannae think to deal with these men without your ability to compel, which you clearly are amiss of since your command has no' made any difference to me." Determination and anger slashed his face. "Your commands will do naught to Gavin as well."

"I'll find a way around the loss of my—" A low branch loomed and she ducked, tried to warn Duncan only—

Thunk. Crash.

His horse, rider-less, sped past and she jerked on her reins.

Behind her, he lay sprawled on the ground and heartbeat pounding, she catapulted off her horse and skidded in beside him. Clutching his leather jerkin, she shook him. "Duncan?"

His breath whooshed out then rasped back in, his eyelashes sluggishly lifting. Groaning, he rubbed the back of his head and muttered, "So that's what Hamish meant by 'watch out for the low branch.'"

"Are you all right?" She cupped his face in her hands, searched his gaze.

"I'm fine, Ella." He pushed her hands away, heaved up, slapped his sides and eyed the trail up ahead.

"You were no' breathing." She stepped in front of him, pressed one hand to his chest, the solid beat making her own steady a little more. "From this moment forth, you will always look where you're riding." Whispered words, and not nearly strong enough to ensure she'd compelled her request of him. "Please, will you do as I say?"

"I always watch the trail when riding, unless I'm arguing with a lass who's determined to do herself harm."

"I have done no harm to myself, while you clearly have, and this isnae the time for a fight." Her horse munched on the long grass growing on one side of the trail, while his steed had ridden off to goodness knows where. "I cannae hear them. Can you?"

The wind whistled through the trees and an owl hooted in the dark. The leaves of the trees rustled and Duncan's breath heaved in and out.

"Nay, but I'll catch them up all the same." He stormed toward her horse, grasped the dangling reins and mounted. Hand thrust out, he gritted his teeth. "I cannae leave you here. Come. We'll ride together since you've now left me with no other choice."

"I've left you with no choice?" Outraged, she slapped his hand away, hoisted herself up onto her mount in front of him, snagged the reins from his hands and slammed her heels into her animal's flanks. "Your horse deserted you. Hold tight. If you fall again, then this time I'll no' return for you."

"I much prefer this whisper of yours to your usual aggravating tone. Have I mentioned that?" With one arm wrapped around her waist, he nipped her ear. Actually nipped her ear. Naught more infuriated her.

"Keep your teeth to yourself, and my usual tone isnae aggravating."

"It surely is." He nipped her ear again.

"Would you stop that." She would have slapped him again only she needed to hold tight to her horse. Racing along the darkened trail through the ever-thickening forest with the most frustrating man she'd ever met at her back, she galloped as fast as the night and the thinning trail would allow. "You are one very annoying man."

"And you're one very incessantly annoying woman. I noticed you're also wearing lad's clothing again. Do you ever wear a gown as a woman does?"

"You said I suited lad's clothing when we met at William's tavern."

"I lied. I prefer my women clothed as women."

"And exactly how many women do you have?"

"I've lost count." A snort in her ear, his breath as hot as the heated wall of his body.

"So I take it you no longer wish to meet me on the first of each month?"

"Did we make such an arrangement?" His grip around her waist tightened.

"I didnae compel you to forget that, or the entire conversation we had. All I asked was that you considered me an annoyance and one you never wished to lay eyes upon again."

"You compelled me to think what I currently think about you?"

"Of course." She shot him a big smile. "Why do you think you hate me so much?"

"Your voice gains in strength. It isnae quite as raspy."

"My voice always rises when anger takes me." Such a shame it still hadn't risen enough to compel him yet. She thundered on down the trail, pine trees thick either side and the damp scent of the earth heavy in the air. "My compelling tone will return afore too long and when it does, I intend to compel you to forget me entirely. That would be most helpful."

"Please do so. Naught would I appreciate more."

"Good. Then 'twill be done."

"Good. I look forward to it." He nipped her ear again. "You might be feisty, but you're also tasty. Ella?" He said her name in a questioning whisper as he smoothed his hands over her hips and along her upper thighs. He splayed his fingers wide and rested his palms there. "I apologize. I've spoken to you most rudely."

"Pardon?"

"I apologize, for demanding you return to the village, for falling from my horse and for worrying you. Yelling at you too. And telling you I look forward to you compelling me to forget you. I also like you clothed just the way you are."

"That is a lot of apologizing."

"Do you forgive me?" He nuzzled her neck and this time nipped the sensitive skin where her shoulder and neck met.

"Nay."

"I dinnae know why I'm touching you like this, or why the urge to keep doing so remains so strong, but you smell so sweet." He breathed deep, his nose tickling her skin. "Like vanilla and fresh air."

"I always add vanilla to my bathwater." Heat flushed her cheeks. Ugh, why had she told him that? "Ignore my babbling."

"Look." He pointed ahead. "The trail comes to an end."

"I see it." The pine trees butted right up to the edge of the cliffs overlooking the sea. The Isle of Raasay was only a few miles wide, and one of the many hundreds of isles along Scotland's western coastline. She pulled her horse to a halt at the cliff's edge and it stamped the dusty ground. Out at sea, moonlight rippled over the white-capped waves and tinged them a golden hue, while farther along the cliffs, a steep trail led down to a narrow beach far below. Horses whinnied, although they remained alone in the dark with no riders in sight.

"You see that?" Duncan motioned toward the scoured lines marking the sand below.

"Gavin must have brought his vessel in here and snuck through the forest before lighting the fires. He's a sneaky one. Ethan's managed to infiltrate his band and attempts to halt his devious attacks, although he's clearly been unable to do so without me and my compelling voice."

"James told me you both do all that you can to honor your father's memory. Peace is what you desire, no' war." He cocked a brow, the wind whipping his black hair into a wind-tossed mess.

"'Tis true, very true." She steered her horse down the tricky cliff side trail, stones scattering over the verge and rapping down the sheer side before plunking into the sand. Duncan tightened his grip on her from behind, his chest flattened to her back and his hips moving in motion with hers as she negotiated the steep downward trail. Such a caressing touch, his entire body rubbing and stimulating hers. Oh my, she could barely breathe with how closely aligned their bodies were, and never had another man ever stirred such an emotion to rise within her before.

Disbelief rocked through her, those emotions ones that should only ever arise should she be with her chosen one. This man couldn't be him. He was a MacKenzie and didn't hold fae blood. She shook her head. Well, as far as she knew he didn't hold fae blood.

"Take care with that last step." His hands came smoothly

around hers on the reins. He tugged and her horse bounded with ease over the craggy edge of the last step and onto the small curve of the beach. With one leg swinging free, he dismounted and landed with a soft clomp on the sand.

She too dismounted and knelt beside him where he crouched to inspect the marks made in the white grains. This thin strip of the beach would likely be covered once the tide rose, the marks completely lost. She touched his arm. "What are your thoughts?"

"These marks arenae as heavy as that of a galley, but no' as light as that of a skiff either. How many men does Gavin have with him?"

"Seven altogether, including himself and Ethan."

"Aye, that number seems about right. 'Tis the number of men I've been chasing."

"You need to cease chasing Gavin. I'll find him and deal with him." She rose and nabbed the dangling reins of the closest horse, led the animal to the trail and clapped a hand on its flank. The mare trotted up the trail and she guided the other horses across and sent each one on up as well. "Gavin is reckless and foolhardy, should never have swiped these horses from the stables, nor set the village alight. He has no thought for others."

"He's far more than foolhardy. He strikes out against the innocent, will learn a lesson to never do so again, the moment I can get my hands on him."

"You need to allow me to impart that lesson." With Duncan's and her horse's reins in hand, she held out his leads to him. "At least I found your horse. Once I catch up to Gavin, 'twould be best if Ethan and I took him straight back to Dunscaith. We'll ensure the Chief of MacDonald learns all about Gavin's misdeeds. Setting Inverarish alight and bringing harm down upon the heads of innocent villagers is unacceptable. The MacDonald cannae argue that fact."

"The MacDonald cares little about facts, has likely

instructed his nephew to wreak the havoc he has upon my land and against those under my care, or have you forgotten I was the one who sailed right into Dunscaith and in doing so caused the war between our clans to escalate?"

"I believe Gavin acts alone, without his chief's knowledge. Please, you need to allow Ethan and I to deal with this. I can speak to Gavin and the MacDonald, ensure all is made right. Surely what is of most importance here is preventing any further blood from being shed, and that I can surely do once my voice has fully returned and I can compel Gavin as needed."

"Can you compel a man to suppress his true nature?"

"Nay, but I can still work some wonders. I'll ensure his chief is made aware of his actions and halts them."

"This war is a deadly one. It takes lives, Ella." He caught her shoulders. "Your voice is naught but a whisper right now and Gavin is a devious man. He'll take full advantage of that, and let's no' forget that this is my battle and no' yours."

"I wasnae asking for your permission to remain on the hunt for Gavin." She mounted her steed and nudged it up the trail in the wake of the other horses.

"I have forty men at my disposal and I can scour the land and seas with far more ability than you can." He bounded onto his saddle and directed his horse up the trail after her. "Gavin will pay for his destruction, something which only I can truly ensure."

"Oh, I'm sure that would be your preference, but it isnae mine." At the top of the cliff, she halted and waited as he joined her. She searched his gaze, the absolute determination flickering across his immoveable. Clearly she'd need to work her fae ability on him a little more, and she could only do that once her compelling tone had returned. For now, it might be best if she kept him close until that moment arrived. Her voice gained a little more in strength with each day that passed, which meant she shouldn't have to remain with him for too long. Aye, that's what she'd do. She also wished to delve deeper into these strange feelings he'd brought forth within her. "I have a request."

"And that is?"

"What if we join together in our hunt for Gavin?"

"You wish to sail with me?"

"I do, provided you can accept a compeller on board your vessel."

"If I agree to your request, then I expect your full obedience to my orders."

"Aye, aye, Captain." Unable to help herself, she saluted him. "Let it also be known though that I expect you to obey my orders as well."

"I follow no lass's orders, and 'tis no wonder I find you so annoying, whether you've compelled that of me or no'." He nudged his horse and moved ahead along the trail.

"'Tis good to see we've finally reached an agreement that suits us both." She cleared her raspy throat and set out after him. The moment she got the full use of her compelling tone back, she'd make him pay for each and every insolent remark he'd just made. The man certainly needed to be brought down a peg or two, and lucky for him, she was completely up for the task.

Up ahead, the horses all trotted in single file and she followed through the forest. When they finally emerged on the hilly rise surrounding the village, she stopped, sat higher in her saddle and surveyed the longhouses lying nestled below within the bay's basin. Some of the villagers still carried the odd pail toward the few tendrils of remaining smoke curling into the air from the burnt homes, although thankfully there appeared to be only severe damage to two of them.

"The fires have been contained." Duncan halted atop his mount beside her.

"I pray no lives were lost."

"As do I." He reached across the small gap between them, caught her hand and squeezed it. "I need to leave this night. Any further delay will only allow Gavin to sail that much farther from my reach. Can you be ready to leave upon our return?"

"Aye, and he sails farther from my reach too."

"How ill have you been?" He lifted her fingers to his lips and kissed the tips before frowning and dropping her hand. "My apologies. I dinnae know what just came over me."

"Think naught of it." Aye, there was more brewing between them than she'd first realized. Knees to her horse's flanks, she guided her mount down the pathway lined with thick grass toward the stables. Ahead, the stable lad swung the gate wide and steered the horses they'd returned with back into the corral. She halted near the high-beamed posts as Duncan trotted in beside her.

"Wait there." He dismounted, gently slapped his horse on the rump and the animal trotted into the corral with the others. He strode around to her, gripped her waist and swung her down beside him. With a nudge, he sent her palfrey along into the corral too. "You didnae answer my question. How ill have you been?"

"I've had a pesky chest illness is all."

"Did you sail your skiff to Raasay?"

"Aye, 'tis beached along the shore no' far from your galley." She pointed to the far rocky end of the shoreline where she'd pulled her boat up onto the sand and secured it to one of the dozen boulders mounded close together.

"I'll have it roped to my galley."

"Thank you." Finding her brother was imperative, and now it appeared she'd be doing so with Duncan leading the venture, or at least until she could compel him as needed then be on her way. Hopefully that would give her enough time to delve deeper into whatever it was that had bloomed between them.

"Ella." He clenched his hands at his sides then growled under his breath and snagged her hand again.

"Is something wrong?"

"An unusual feeling assails me."

"As in…" She touched one finger to his pursed lips squeezed so tightly together.

"You make me feel out of sorts."

"In what way?" He made her feel exactly the same. Allowing herself a certain freedom, she gently traced along his lips, softly back and forth and a hungry growl rumbled from deep within his chest, one which caused a strange heat to gather in her own core and surge through her, a heat that also made her heart beat faster and her soul lift higher. She stroked down over the cleft in his chin then dipped to the V of his white tunic. His black leather jerkin lay fastened loosely overtop of his shirt, the tails flapping free underneath. More emotions arose within her. Surprise and shock coursed strongly, but so too did desire. She touched him so freely, and he'd touched her so freely as well. Such shouldn't feel so right unless she stood with her chosen one. More and more, the signs pointed to a mated bond having formed between them, only how?

Driven to test these new emotions further, she reached up on the tips of her toes and pushed her hands through the silky softness of his black hair. Touching him made her belly flutter, this moment one she didn't wish to have ever end.

"What are you doing?" He snagged her wayward hands, pressed them to his cheeks and rubbed his skin against her palms. "Hell, and what am I doing? You're naught more than an annoyance to me."

"Aye, I am, as you are for me."

* * * *

Perhaps he'd taken a far harder knock to the head when he'd fallen than he'd realized. Never had another woman ever brought such fierce and hungry emotions to blazing life within him. Only why Ella Matheson? She was a compeller with the ability to command his very thoughts, of which she'd already done a number of times. He stepped back from her, gave her a firm nod. "We should leave. Do you have all you need?"

"I left my bag at the inn when I first arrived, afore the fires were lit. I'll go and collect it." She stepped away, a soft smile lighting her eyes before she turned and disappeared inside the stone inn next to the stables.

Candlelight glowed from the inn's windows and a puff of smoke swirled from the chimney and floated away on the nighttime breeze. From the first day he'd seen her atop Dunscaith's battlements she'd intrigued him and now, even more so. This woman held strong fae blood, just as he did through his mother's line, not that he could ever allow her to learn of that secret. So few knew the truth and that's the way it needed to remain.

Aye, eight years of age he'd been when he and his twin brother had first learnt the truth about their heritage. Their father's second-in-command had rapped on the door and awoken him and Coll in the middle of the night, told them a woman of fae blood awaited them downstairs and that their father had called for them to attend him immediately. They'd pulled on breeches under their bed-shirts, tugged socks on and trekked downstairs to their father's solar on the lower floor of the keep.

Father had pushed an ink bottle and quill to the center of his desk, perched on the front edge and eyed him and Coll as he'd gestured to the woman with a wee lass hiding within her skirts. *"Coll, Duncan, this is Mistress Grace from the fae village. She brings you a message you must heed."*

"More than a message." With a tender smile, the woman with a gentle voice had lowered to her knees before them. *" 'Tis so good to see you both. You must be Coll?"* She'd grasped Coll's hands and smiled wider at him. *"Your brown eyes are flecked with gold, just as they were at your birth."*

"Grace." Father had thumped one fisted hand on his desk and rattled the dagger resting near the edge. *"Tell them what you've seen and no more."*

"They must learn the full truth in order to heed my word, unless you wish for the death of your sons." None had ever defied Father before, but Mistress Grace appeared ready to do so. Intrigued, he'd listened well.

"You intend to speak more in-depth about Beth?" Father had asked her.

"I must in this case."

"Damn it." Father had fisted his hands then muttered, *"Fine. Say what you will. None within this solar will utter a word after you've left. My sons shall do as I command them."*

"Thank you." Mistress Grace glanced between him and his brother. *"I hold the fae skill of death-warning and can receive visions. Of those who live but are soon to die, I can warn them aforehand and ensure they are given the chance to live. Earlier this eve, I had a vision of both of you."*

"I remember you," Coll had piped up. *"You cared for us when we were little."*

An image of this woman flickered through Duncan's mind, one of her tending to their scraped knees as wee lads and reciting bedtime stories before tucking them into their beds and slipping outside their door to her own chamber next to theirs.

"I remember you too." Memories from his earlier years continued to surge forth. Mistress Grace had been so loving and kind, a nurse with a tender hand, a most worthy guardian as well. *"I'm Duncan. What have you seen, Mistress Grace?"*

"More than I wish, I'm afraid." She cleared her throat. *"In order to ensure your survival you must both listen to me well. From this day forth, neither of you must ever raise a hand in battle against a Matheson, not because you willnae be strong warriors, but because in harming a Matheson you will also be harming yourselves. Soon, you will both understand what I speak of, for there will be things you'll be able to do that no other MacKenzie warrior can. The fae battle skill will come upon you and when it does your strength will be immense."*

"We're MacKenzies, no' Mathesons. How can we hold a fae skill?" Coll had glanced at Father, and so had Duncan. *"Mother was a MacLennan and no' of fae blood."*

"What's going on, Father?" Such confusion had swarmed Duncan.

"I never wished to speak of this, no' since you both took your mother's death so hard."

"Cait MacLennan has passed?" Shock had coursed across Mistress Grace's face as she'd risen to her feet

"Aye, she took a terrible illness last winter. She's been gone for nigh on a year now." Father shoved off his desk and paced the solar then halted before him and Coll. *"Since I no longer have any choice but to speak of this, I shall. Cait wasnae your true mother. Afore your birth, I handfasted with a fae lass named Beth, although she passed away while birthing you both. Mistress Grace was here at the time of your true mother's passing and she took care of you until 'twas time for her to return to her own people at the village. The knowledge of your fae blood isnae something I speak of, ever, and neither of you are permitted to speak of it either, or your coming skill."* The war braids plaited at each side of Father's head had swayed as he'd lowered to his haunches. *"You are my sons, hold my blood, and your additional strength will be attributed to that fact alone. Do you both understand? I certainly cannae lose the alliance I've formed with the MacLennan, or the land I've come by."*

"Aye, Father," both he and Coll had murmured, shock still coursing through them both. All he'd ever known had been a lie. His mother had been of fae blood, and now he and Coll would soon hold the fae battle skill. Along with the wave of shock came a flare of awe. Aye, he'd soon hold a skill, as those from clan Matheson did. Incredible.

"There is more," Mistress Grace continued, the plea in her eyes clear to see as she'd eyed Father. *"You must ensure Coll and Duncan are taught the arts of warfare well. One day, far in*

the future, they will meet a fae sorceress by the name of Muirin and her brother, a seer named Hamish. I saw them both in my vision. They are the ones who'll ensure your sons fulfil their destiny."

"What destiny?"

"All I can say is, 'tis time for the fae to live."

To this day, twenty years on, Grace's decree still rumbled through his mind, for he and Coll had met Muirin and Hamish only a few years after they'd left Father's keep and taken control of their own strongholds on Loch Carron. Over the past few years, Muirin and Hamish had been instrumental in aiding him and Coll in strengthening their battle skill, and now they intended to fulfil the rest of their destiny. 'Twas time for the fae to live, which included him and Coll. Never would he allow Gavin MacDonald to take from them what they'd worked so hard to gain.

With a deep breath, he strode back along the grassy verge of the pebbly shoreline. A few of his men and the villagers continued to dampen the ashes with pails of water and he halted next to James and Hamish as they stood conversing.

Hamish eyed his forehead. "I see you didnae duck in time."

"And you could have elaborated more about why I had to." He shook his head. That argument could keep for another time. "Thankfully I found Ella, although Gavin unfortunately escaped us. He and his men abandoned their horses across the other side of Raasay and set sail. I didnae see them out on the water, although they cannae have sailed far. Ella has asked if she might join us during our hunt and I've agreed since I'd rather keep a closer eye on her." He grasped James's shoulder. "I'll send supplies and men to aid in the rebuild once I return to Ardan House, but for now we must be away."

"Your aid in the rebuild would be greatly appreciated." James nodded.

"'Twill be done. Be assured of that." To Hamish, he said,

"Rope Ella's skiff to our galley."

"Will do." Stepping backward as he left, his second grinned with a mischievous smile. "She's a feisty lass that one. Our coming travels will surely be most interesting with her on board."

"More than interesting." Of that he didn't doubt. Teeth gritted, he walked toward his men and once they'd gathered around him, he cleared his throat. "Ella Matheson will be sailing with us. The lass is of fae blood and still recovering from an illness which took her voice. She wishes to find her brother who sails with Gavin and will remain under my protection until I say otherwise."

"If her brother sails with Gavin, does that no' make her our enemy as well?" Ivor, his claymore glinting at his side, cast his narrowed gaze toward the inn as Ella appeared on the front step. "My laird, the compeller may have ended the battle at Dunscaith which we fought, but with her ability she could still so easily send us all to our death."

"Hamish has *seen* that she seeks only to find and aid her brother in halting Gavin in his misdeeds. She desires only to seek peace, no' war." The need to defend Ella and ensure his men understood her true nature rose strongly within him. "Am I understood?"

"Aye, my laird." A firm nod from Ivor and the remainder of his men around him. All followed his orders, for if they didn't they'd instead earn his wrath.

"Take a dip and wash up. We leave immediately, the moment everyone is once again on board."

His men dispersed and Ella stepped in beside him, a buttery-yellow leather vest now donned overtop of her tan tunic, her black leather breeches still clinging snugly to her shapely legs. Knee-high leather boots encased her calves and with her Matheson tartan tossed over one shoulder and her traveling sack over the other, she appeared a vision, one that made him catch his breath.

"I've informed my men that you're joining us."

"They may no' appreciate having a Matheson on board, but I'd never harm them. I'd like to make that clear to them."

"I already have." He held out his hand for her bag and she passed it to him. He lobbed it to Ivor who'd bounded on board and the man stowed it under the rear bench seat.

She stepped into the surf and he scooped her up before the incoming waves splashed her. "Put me down."

"Nay, there's no need for you to get wet." With her clasped close to his chest, he walked through the knee-deep water and swung her over the side onto his vessel.

Hands on her hips, she glared at him and he couldn't help but chuckle as he boosted himself in. "Cease laughing at me, Duncan."

"You agreed to following my orders, and you appear ready to complain about them already."

"I agreed under duress."

"I dinnae recall any duress, my grumpy one."

"And cease calling me your grumpy one. That is the second time you've done so."

"When was the first?"

"At William's tavern when you attempted to dance with me."

"Aye, well I dinnae quite have the best recollection of that night since you compelled me to forget some of it and then altered the rest."

"I only compelled you to think of me as naught more than an annoyance. There is naught else you should truly have forgotten." She jabbed him in the chest. "Cease toying with me."

"I like toying with you. You make a worthy opponent." He steered her down the center aisle, settled her on the rear bench seat beside him and shouted to his men as they boarded, "All to oars. I intend on finding Gavin MacDonald this night and ensuring he pays for his attacks against us. We shall seek our retribution."

A hearty roar sounded from his men and they nabbed their oars, dunked them into the water while he gripped the rudder and guided them out of the bay.

"You are impossible," Ella whispered. Arms crossed, she glared at him then stared out over the night-shrouded seas. "I truly wish I could have said that loud enough for it to have been more effective."

"I understand that I frustrate you." To Hamish, he called out, "Raise the sail."

His man nabbed the ropes and unfurled the sail. The wind slapped into it and sent them cruising through the inky waters of the sound, the moon hazy as it slid behind a thick layer of stormy cloud.

"You more than frustrate me." Shivering, she tugged her tartan from over her shoulder and wrapped it around her. "'Tis getting colder."

"I have a fur if you have need of it?"

"T-this is f-fine." Her teeth chattered, her lips going suddenly blue.

"You should have said you were cold." He couldn't stand to see her so chilled. From underneath the bench, he foraged within his supplies and pulled out his fur. With the thick brown pelt in hand, he enveloped her in its warmth and tucked it in nice and tight under her chin. "Is that better?"

"Aye, but I wish I could say nay then see what you'd do next."

"I'd offer you my body to warm you with." Grinning, he lifted his fur higher at the back of her neck so it blocked the wind from behind.

"Do you flirt with all the lasses like this?"

"Nay, only you."

"Then it appears I'm the lucky one." Frowning, she

wriggled closer to him on the bench. "Tell me more about Coll. I'm aware he's your twin and the eldest."

"What do you wish to know?"

"I may know of him, but I've never met him. Can one tell the two of you apart?"

"We're the same height and build, evenly matched in strength, although there are enough differences to tell us apart."

"Like?"

"Coll's eyes are the same shade as yours, brown flecked with gold, whereas mine are a plain shade of blue."

"Your eyes are a stunning shade of blue." She snuck one hand out from within the fur, touched her palm to his cheek and looked deeper into his eyes. "They're a warm blue, as vibrant in color as a clear summer's sky. They're also the same shade as my brother's and my mama's eyes. I've always wished mine were such a pretty color."

"My eyes arenae pretty." He'd never live it down if any of his men heard that comment. 'Twas just as well her voice couldn't travel any farther than the two of them.

"They're most definitely pretty, but in a very rugged sort of way." She giggled. "You are just like Ethan. Whenever I call his blue eyes pretty, he acts as if I've just struck him."

"I'm a warrior."

"So I noticed." She stroked her fingers back and forth along his cheek, a mischievous tilt lifting her lips. "Aye, you're a very pretty warrior indeed."

"You are the worst tease, and I clearly shouldnae have offered you my aid."

"You didnae offer. I asked to join you." She buried her nose in his neck, her next whispered words sending his pulse racing, "What secrets are you hiding from me, Duncan MacKenzie?"

"None." He should insert some space between them, only he couldn't move. Having her this close made his heart thump harder and every protective instinct within him roar to the forefront.

"Aye, you are, and I wish I could compel the truth from you, but that will have to wait until my voice is fully restored, unless of course you wish to share the truth with me on your own." She kissed his neck and he barely remained seated. All he wanted to do was topple her into the planked boards underfoot and demand she kiss him proper.

"Sit back where you should." The air suddenly stilled and the sail went limp. Up ahead, fog swirled as they neared the Isle of Skye, although he couldn't make out the land with the veiled mist thickening by the second.

"Everything within me demands I get even closer to you and there can be only one answer for such an intense emotion to take me." She searched his gaze.

"Which would be?" They glided right into the fog and it smothered them.

"For you to be my chosen one, only for that to be so, you'd have to hold fae blood."

"My father is Colin MacKenzie, my mother the late Cait MacLennan. Neither have ever held your Matheson fae blood."

"Yet I am still drawn to you, which is the way of those who are mated." The gold at the edge of her beautiful brown eyes glimmered bright. "Those who are soul bound wait for their chosen one, and if you are my mate as I believe you might be, then you must have been waiting for me too. Am I right? Have you found it difficult to dally with another? Are you the one I seek, Duncan MacKenzie?"

"Nay, and I never shall be." He couldn't allow her to believe they were mated. So too should his men believe a bond had formed between them, then his fae blood would be exposed. They cruised deeper into the ever-thickening fog and his men dunked their oars deep and rowed while next to him, Ella shivered within the chilly mist. He wrapped an arm around her back and drew her closer to his side. Aye, he couldn't be her chosen one, because that would certainly let loose a slew of trouble he had no intention of allowing.

Chapter 3

Sweet sensations flittered through Ella as Duncan wrapped an arm around her and tucked her closer to his side. The fog continued to thicken until she couldn't see more than a few feet in any direction. Certainly his men on board weren't visible anymore, only the splashing of their oars dunking into the water proved they remained close by. She rubbed her cheek against Duncan's shoulder, snuck her fingers between the front ties of his black leather jerkin and traced over the hard muscles of his chest covered in a soft layer of fine white cotton. Aye, this man more than intrigued her. "Do you feel it?" she whispered to him.

"Ella, you need to cease touching me the way that you are." He covered her hand with his and halted her movement.

"Something draws us closer together, and I'm no' imagining it."

"That something would be called your brother and your current search for him and Gavin MacDonald." With the fog smothering them, he rose to his feet and tried to peer through it across the waves. "I sense we're getting closer to Skye's shoreline and I've no wish to sail into the rocks."

"Go if you must. I understand."

"I'll return soon. Stay right here." He strode into the soupy mist and disappeared.

Something sloshed over her shoulder and she wriggled around. Her skiff was tied to the stern only naught was visible other than the rope secured to it.

"'Tis about time my laird left you alone." A hand clamped around her mouth then another around her leg. "Can you swim, lass? The shoreline is close, a mere few strokes away. I apologize, but I cannae have you compel us to our death, which will surely happen should you remain." He tossed her overboard and she splashed into the darkened depths and went down.

Something scraped over her head. The hull of her skiff. Hands shoved up, she pushed against the underside and sank deeper and only once assured her boat had passed safely overhead did she kick free of Duncan's fur and heave back up to the surface.

Stupid cloying fog, and stupid lost voice. She couldn't even yell and alert those on board she'd gone over. Which of his men had thought to do her harm? Clearly whoever it was feared her fae skill and what she could do, just as so many did. She let out a long sigh, so not surprised. With only a few uttered words she could send a man to his death, not that she ever would. Never mind. She'd swim to shore and continue on with her mission regardless of Duncan and his men, her lost skiff too. She'd been caught in worse situations.

She rolled onto her back, scooped water at her sides and tried to get her bearings. The moon, a mere pinprick of light through the hazy gloom above, did naught to aid her or light her way. She rolled over and kicked in what better be the right direction.

With sure strokes, she swam at a good pace until a playful seal pup darted around and underneath her. The waters in these parts teemed with wildlife, which included some sea creatures she had no wish to meet, or become a tasty meal to. Goodness. The warrior had said the shoreline was close, a mere few strokes away. It clearly wasn't.

With the cold water penetrating deep into her bones, she tried to kick harder but with each stroke her arms slapped heavier into the water and her legs, so chilled and numb, became no help at all.

Hot tears pressed behind her eyes and her greatest fear rose with striking force. Her death, and leaving Mama and Ethan to cope with the turmoil of their grief. That kind of heartache wasn't something she'd ever allow them to go through, not after they'd already lost Papa. She had to make it to land, wherever that dratted land was. She floated, the waves washing over her and salt stinging her lips and cheeks. The tide moved her and waves crashed somewhere up ahead. Land. Finally. She'd almost made it.

A wave crashed and she got washed up onto a cluster of rocks. Heaving to her feet, she stumbled to keep herself upright. Over the slickness, she clambered then staggered onto a pebbly beach. Shudders raked through her. Keep moving. She had to find shelter, mayhap within those trees swaying so very close. She walked and wobbled, black spots dancing before her eyes. Only a few more steps.

* * * *

Pain slammed through Duncan's chest and he stumbled to his knees at the bow where he maintained a lookout for the rocks bordering Skye's coastline. 'Twas as if someone had taken a sword and thrust it straight through his chest. He patted his heart to make sure no one had, the erratic beat burning and making him gasp for air.

"Duncan?" Hamish hauled him up by the arm. "Are you all right?"

"I—I—" Ella's face wavered before his eyes, as if the pain wasn't his, but hers. He lurched through the fog to the end of the galley and searched for her. Hell. Where was she? "Ella!" He bellowed her name. "Damn it, Ella. Answer me!"

Only the slapping of the waves against the sides of his vessel broke the silence.

"All eyes on the water," he yelled to his men. "Ella's gone overboard."

The wind lifted, sent tendrils of the hazy mist swirling, enough that he caught sight of the rocks bordering Skye's craggy shoreline. He turned the rudder and sent them directly toward land where the surf washed into the bay. They crested a wave, the hull scraping the sandy sea floor and as it did, he bounded over the side along with a score of his men. He searched the crashing waves where they came into shore, his heartbeat a raging mess, his men right beside him as they searched as well.

"There!" From the bow, Hamish pointed toward the darkened tree line.

Ella lay sprawled on the grassy verge and he bounded through the surf and sprinted across, dropped down beside her and tipped her back over onto her back. Her hair lay tangled around her face, her skin ashen and her lips an icy blue with barely a whisper of breath moving from her mouth. She was cold. Too cold. "Bring me as many blankets as you can and get a fire lit," he yelled to Ivor, the closest of his men running toward him.

"Will do." Ivor skidded in the sand, turned back and raced to the galley being hauled the last few feet into shore.

Gently, he scooped Ella up and carried her toward a more sheltered area under the trees while his men saw to the fire. Sticks caught alight and flames soared as they built the heat. Hamish tossed several logs onto the crackling blaze and Duncan laid Ella down as close as he dared to the flames, wrapped her tight in his arms and rubbed her back. "Wake up, Ella."

"I've got what you need." Ivor bounded back, spread blankets and furs over him and Ella and tucked them tight. "Does she breathe?"

"Aye, but barely." He had no choice left to him and

underneath the layers piled over him, he tugged Ella's wet clothing off, her riding boots, tunic and breeches. She likely wouldn't appreciate that he'd done so, but sharing his body warmth with her right now was imperative. Even his men understood that, wouldn't question his decision to strip her and do so. She was under his protection and he wouldn't fail her now, or at least not again as he'd just done.

Once he'd stripped them both, he stuck her frozen fingers between them and clamped his legs either side of her legs. Skin against skin, he warmed her as best as he could, the heat of the fire penetrating through the blankets and warming them further.

Hamish wrung out their wet clothes and tossed them over the branches of the closest tree before handing him a skin. "'Tis whiskey. Make sure she gets some of it down."

"She needs more than whiskey." He lifted the skin to Ella's lips and dribbled a little of it into her mouth. She gagged but got some down and he took a swig himself, then nodded at his man. "It might be a long night."

"I'll keep the fire burning, as well as ensure our men patrol this area. This is MacDonald land and we'll need to take every precaution while seeking shelter on it."

"Mayhap Gavin and his men too were forced to seek shelter as we have." None could sail far in such a heavy fog.

"I'll remain alert for a vision, will send out some teams to search the coastline immediately." Hamish disappeared within the foggy haze, his men dispersing as well although a small guard remained near his beached galley to watch over them.

"Ella, open your eyes for me, please." He tucked the covers over their heads to keep the warmth fully inside, the fire's light penetrating through with a reddish-orange glow. She released the softest sigh against his chest then wriggled closer. "That's it, seek the warmth you need from me. I'll always offer it."

"You arenae dressed and neither am I," she grizzled, her husky words barely audible but easing the tightness within his chest all the same.

"That's right, my grumpy one. Keep talking to me."

"I'm no' your grumpy one." She moaned again then rubbed her cold nose across his chest. "Well, actually I might be grumpy at the moment, and how on earth are you so warm when that water was so dreadfully cold?"

"'Twas no' cold for me, no' when I train daily in the sea." He swam several miles at the break of dawn each day, no matter the season. "A number of my men have left to search the coastline for Gavin. If he and Ethan are here, we'll find them."

"Dinnae let any of them hurt Ethan."

"None of my men would ever harm one of the fae. You can be assured of that." He caressed down her back, stroked over her smooth bottom and pulled her even closer against him.

"You are getting rather familiar with me, Duncan MacKenzie." She snuck one hand out from between them and swatted his backside. "You need to cease touching me where you've no right to touch me, unless I say you can."

"For now, I'll touch you wherever I please." Such relief poured through him, her grumpiness soothing him beyond belief. "Put your hand back between us. I've no wish for you to lose your fingers due to the cold."

"My fingers are perfectly fine where they are." Still, she did as he'd commanded her and snuck her hand back between them. With her nose buried in his neck, she nipped his flesh.

His cock twitched and hardened, his blood pounding and his need for her rising so swiftly.

"I can feel you," she breathed raggedly. "And I mean that part of you prodding into me."

"That prodding is an expected reaction when a man is forced to hold a woman so close while wearing naught. Ignore my arousal."

"How do I ignore that? You've a rather large, well, it's rather large by the feel of it." She wriggled some more, her squirms only making him harden further.

"Staying still might help." Gritting his teeth, he kissed the top of her head. "Please."

"I'm starting to feel quite hot." Within the darkness of the covers, she looked into his eyes, the fire's glow which penetrated through lighting the gold sparks gleaming within the heavenly shade of brown. "Push the covers back a little, please."

"I'll decide when you're hot enough."

"Have you ever been aroused this way with another lass afore?" She arched a brow. "Be honest with me, because those who are mated can barely tolerate the touch of another and the feel of you against me is rather thrilling, no matter my growling."

"Damn it, Ella. We arenae mated."

"So you say, but so I disagree. I've never felt such a deep desire for another as I do for you, although for you to be my mate would mean you're hiding your fae blood from me. I also did no' fall into the water. Someone tossed me overboard, right before apologizing for having to do so. One of your men fears that I might compel you all to your death."

"There isnae a man on board my galley who'd toss an innocent lass into the sea."

"Yet someone did." She cupped his cheeks in her hands and murmured, "Many of our fae-blooded kind are soul bound to another, and when we come of age and find our chosen one, we join together in all ways, the silken strands between our souls fully weaving together into one. 'Tis a bond we desire, hope with all our heart is gifted to us. I can sense that bond taking form right now between us."

"There is no bond forming, no matter how much you wish for it."

"The odd marriage has taken place between our clans over the years. Are you certain you dinnae hold even a trace of fae blood, that it does no' flow within your father or mother's line somehow?"

"Beyond certain."

"Then mayhap you're unaware of that fae blood." She touched one finger to his lower lip, swept it from corner to corner with a soft sigh escaping her lips. "Could I ask a request of you?"

"That depends on what it might be."

"Would you kiss me?"

* * * *

Never in Ella's life had her heart beat this fast, or her desire risen to such a staggering need. Surely she wasn't the only one feeling these incredibly new and wonderful emotions. "I want you to kiss me, to know what it's like to share the same breath as you."

"You truly are an annoyance, one I wish I'd never laid eyes upon, whether you compelled that of me or no'."

Fierce need rushed through her and she pushed him onto his back and scrambled on top. "There is something growing between us and you must give it a chance to take a firm hold. Damn well kiss me now, or else I'll kiss you."

"Are you always this demanding?"

"I am this night." She leaned closer, her lips a mere breath away from his as she whispered, "Surely one kiss willnae hurt you."

"How about you kiss me instead?"

"Agreed." She would get the truth out of him somehow, but for now, she would allow the ties between them to continue to strengthen and deepen, for him to see that none could halt the mated bond when it took form, not him, and certainly not her. She licked his lower lip, wanted so much more, and she took. She kissed him, their mouths joined and his breath mingling so sweetly with hers. Clearly one kiss wouldn't be enough. She delved deeper, urged his lips farther apart and kissed him with all the fierce need roaring to full and vibrant life within her.

"Ella." He murmured her name, clamped her backside tight and kissed her just as greedily as she kissed him, his hips rocking against hers and his shaft a hard rod of steel poking into her belly.

"I like your kisses, Duncan. I want more of them." She molded her body to his, left not one inch of them separated.

"You are clearly intent on ravishment."

"Aye, I am this night." She couldn't keep her smile at bay. "We will make a good match, no matter you're a MacKenzie and I'm a Matheson."

"I willnae take advantage of an innocent lass in the dark of the night, and while on enemy soil no less." He rolled her over under the furs, came up over her and kissed her with a breathless urgency that thrummed through her too. "Ella." He skimmed her sides, slid his hands under her. "Dinnae encourage me any further."

"When you're ready to trust me with your secrets, then I'll be here." She seized his biceps and kissed him again, passionately, until the heat between them blazed and swarmed her senses.

"Have to stop," he muttered as he lifted his head. Panting, he rolled off her and onto his back, pushed the covers clear of their heads and peered through the thick fog.

Mayhap they should stop. They were on his enemy's soil and two of his men remained close. She could just make them out where they kept guard near his half-beached galley.

"I want you to close your eyes and rest." Firm words, his gaze unarguable as he faced her on his side.

"Only if you stay with me."

"Of course." He grumbled some more under his breath and she snuggled against him, the blankets a haven a warmth surrounding her, just as his presence was.

Slowly, she drifted, never more at peace than at this moment. Aye, he was her chosen one, and of that she no longer had any doubt. Only now, she needed to make him see so as well.

Ha. That might just be her greatest mission to come.

* * * *

A seagull screeched overhead and Ella stirred awake as a soft breeze rose. She stretched and pushed the covers back off her head and smiled. The skies had lightened, dawn close and the cloying fog beginning to swirl away. The misty silhouette of Duncan's two guards standing on patrol near the galley became clearer, while at her side her mate snoozed and although he'd denied their bond last eve, she'd never have fallen asleep so readily beside him if he didn't hold the other half of her soul. Smiling wider, she ran her fingers through his black locks and touched her nose to his. "Wake up, my stubborn one."

"I need more sleep," he muttered and hooked his arms around her waist. "It cannae be morning yet."

"'Tis close and we must dress afore your men return."

"Dress, aye." He blinked his eyes open, kissed her forehead then grumbled loud and long as he sat up and reached behind him. He snagged his satchel next to the fire and grumbled some more. "I shouldnae be kissing you."

"You're clearly no' a morning person."

"I simply find it annoying to wake up next to you." He foraged within his bag, pulled out a tunic and eased the soft blue cotton over his head then thrust a pair of brown rawhide breeches under the covers and shuffled into them. Once dressed, he slipped out, stuffed his feet into his boots and sheathed his claymore at his side before passing across her bag someone had kindly thought to leave for her. "Hamish hung your wet clothes on the branch behind you. Dinnae forget to collect them."

"Thank you." She flipped open the top flap of her bag, pulled out her blue breeches and cream tunic, shoved them under the blankets and dressed while he turned his gaze away. "We might be mated, but clearly 'tis too dangerous for me to stay here with you when one of your men tossed me overboard. Even though he apologized for having to do so, I must still leave. I cannae take the risk to my life, no' when Ethan needs me, my mama too."

She shuffled out of their warm cocoon, tugged her riding boots on and slid her dagger inside an ankle sheath.

"I've already told you that none of my men would dare harm a lass. You must be mistaken."

"I understand your loyalty belongs to your men, and rightly so." She couldn't fault him for his trust in his men. "Although there have simply been too many years of warring between our clans that cannae be forgiven or forgotten. So many fear my skill as well, particularly when 'tis well known I could kill a man if I wished, and with only one word."

"I've given you my vow of protection."

"I'm most grateful for it, but it isnae enough at present."

"You're remaining here with me, and I'll have it no other way."

"Spoken like a true mate." On her toes, she smiled and kissed his cheek. "Mayhap we'll continue this conversation later. I require a few moments of privacy so I might tend to my needs."

"Of course, although dinnae wander too far." He stormed down toward his guardsmen.

Wonderful. It appeared she'd been gifted with the most stubborn mate there was. She slung her black coat on and once wrapped within its warmth, ducked into the trees. She trekked a hundred feet inland then once she'd found a thick bush, crouched behind it. Done, she walked back to the beach and washed her hands at the water's edge.

Duncan still stood with his two guardsmen, his arms crossed over his wide chest while behind him the sun breached the horizon and sent a heavenly wash of gold and pink streaming through the pale blue sky. The ocean's skyline outlined him to perfection, her warrior who was armed and ready for the trials of the day to come. Unfortunately, she'd likely continue to be one of them.

She plodded to her bag and sat, pulled out an oatcake and ate. As she finished her meager meal, a team of his men trekked out of the woods with a dozen fish hanging from a long stick between them.

Two of the men set their catch over the fire, added more logs to keep it ablaze while the others dispersed about the beach, some washing up where the waves tumbled into shore and others perching on low boulders along the grassy verge of the bank. None cast her any strange looks or seemed overly worried about her. Who on earth had decided to do her harm? If she could pinpoint the man, 'twould make things far easier.

Another team of men returned, the warrior at the head holding clear Viking heritage, his pale hair shining a golden-white in the morning sun and his legs as thick as tree trunks.

"Ivor!" Duncan hailed the man over and the Viking joined him. Gripping the man's shoulder, Duncan asked, "Did you find aught?"

"We tramped to the village at the tip of Loch Ainort, spoke to a lad who said no fog had descended on them. The boy had caught sight of a vessel out on the water during the night, one holding six or seven men. It sailed on down Loch na Cairidh toward the Isle of Scalpay. Once we learnt of this, we turned and tramped back."

"That'll be Gavin MacDonald for sure. We'll break our fast and sail directly to Scalpay, see if we can spy him there. The others willnae be far away so break your fast now afore we leave."

"How does the lass fare this morn?" Ivor glanced her way, worry swirling within his striking green eyes.

"She fares far better than she did last eve, although has declared one of my men tossed her overboard, right afore apologizing to do so. Keep a listening ear out for any dissension amongst the ranks. I dinnae believe one of my men would ever harm her, but should that no' be the case, then I'll have that man's head for what he's done."

"Aye, my laird. I'll keep out a listening ear."

"Good." Duncan walked away from Ivor and crouched next to the fire. He tore some of the cooked fish free and ate as he eyed her.

A standoff. She could handle such from him.

Another team of men returned with plucked geese swinging from their hands and they skewered the meat onto sturdy sticks and propped it over a rack to cook.

"You appear hearty and hale this morn, a welcoming sight for certain." Smiling, Hamish dropped in beside her, having appeared right out of the woods. "Is all well?"

"Aye, I'm much better, although I wouldnae mind getting my voice fully back." Whispering all the time wore on her.

Leaning closer, he murmured, "Your ability to compel shall come and go this day, then be far more reliant by this eve." A knowing glimmer flickered in his gaze. "Give Duncan some time. He's no' yet ready to accept you and your bond."

"You've *seen* that what I've said is true?"

"Glimpses here and there, but enough to confirm you two are in fact soul bound." He patted her leg, this fae-blooded seer now possibly her greatest ally. "I'll do what I can to aid you in your mission with him."

"More so I'd rather have your aid in another matter. I was tossed overboard last eve, didnae fall at all. The man apologized first, clearly fears me and what I can do. Did you see aught?"

"Nay, and like most fae seers, I dinnae always see all."

"I understand." 'Twas the same for Nessa, the seer within their village. She tucked the rest of her belongings away in her satchel, pushed to her feet and nodded at Hamish. "Do excuse me."

"Of course." He nodded and headed across to the fire,

plucked some meat from one skewer and leaned against a tree to eat.

Time for her to go. She walked down toward the shoreline where her skiff sat beached on the sand near the galley.

"Ella." Duncan stormed after her. "Where are you going?"

"I'm leaving, as we discussed."

"Nay, you'll be staying, as we discussed."

She rested one hand on his chest. "I need to continue my search for Gavin, although I can no longer remain on board your vessel to do so. Our time to part has come." Aye, her mate would continue to deny their bond unless she perhaps forced him to see the truth. Their coming separation would aid him with that, as well as ensure her safety by distancing herself from the warrior who'd thought to do her harm. She stepped away, tossed her bag on board the skiff and shoved her boat into the water.

"You cannae leave." He grasped her arms.

"I can and I am." She cleared her throat, pushed harder with her voice to raise it higher and prayed her compelling tone would come forth. "You will allow me to leave without any hinder." Her voice rang with authority, with an unmistakably hypnotic demand. Thank goodness. "I will always be an annoyance to you, until you choose to see the truth about our bond and accept it."

His blue eyes clouded over under her compulsion, one he couldn't fight.

"Close your eyes, Duncan, then count to one-hundred, nice and slow, and once you're done you may open your eyes again." His long lashes fluttered down and carefully, she slid her arms free of his tight grip, kissed his cheek and murmured, "I wish you a safe journey. You may begin the count."

"One, two, three..." Hands fisted at his sides, he rocked where he stood, the burnished hilt of his massive two-handed claymore glinting at his side.

She shoved her skiff deeper into the water, clambered on

board and with the oars in hand, rowed from the center seat. Once she'd cleared the surf, she raised the sail and took one last look at her chosen one still standing on the beach, his eyes closed and teeth gritted.

Hopefully, he'd forgive her for what she'd just done, would come to his senses afore too long as well. Aye, leaving him right now was her only option, no matter doing so pained her to the very depths of her soul.

Chapter 4

"Four, five, six." Eyes shut, Duncan growled under his breath. Counting was the last thing he wished to do when all he wanted was to chase Ella and bring her back to his side, only breaking her compelling demand was damn impossible. "Seven, eight, nine."

"Duncan?" Hamish's voice wafted over him.

"Give me a moment." What blasted number was he up to? "Ten," he muttered, eyes still squeezed shut, the compulsion to count overriding all else. "Eleven, twelve…" Endlessly, he continued on. "Ninety-nine, one-hundred."

He reached the magic number and opened his eyes, dragged in a deep breath then growled at his second-in-command. "Speak to me."

"Are you feeling well?" Hamish stared at him as if he'd grown another head.

"Ella wanted to leave, so I let her." His gut roiled into a seething mess. Out at sea, she'd already rounded the tip of the bay and disappeared from his sight. "She insists one of my men tossed her overboard and that she's safest away from me." Around the fire and along the grassy verge, his men broke their fast. Each and every one had stood staunchly at his side during the war that had raged these past years. He couldn't separate any one of them out as the possible culprit.

"I never *saw* anyone wish her any harm, but right now we need to focus more on what she's clearly compelled of you. If you wish to fight her compulsion, then you must look inside your heart for the truth." Hamish grasped his shoulder. "How do you truly feel about her?"

"She's forced our separation."

"You have no' been forthcoming with her. Mayhap 'tis time you shared the knowledge of how you came to hold fae blood with her. She is blood kin to me and I can assure you, she can be trusted."

"No one knows about my fae blood other than you and those I trust implicitly."

"Do you no' wish to claim her as yours?"

"How can I when that would release my secret?" Even he could no longer ignore the signs that they were soul bound, but that made little difference when he had kin to protect. He expelled a long breath, tried to calm his aggrieved thoughts. The surf washed into shore and the sun rose higher and glimmered over the blue-green surface and as it did, his mate sailed even farther away from him, so far now beyond his reach.

"You are the son of a chief, and none would ever dispute your decision to take her for yourself so you might ensure her strong fae blood flowed directly within your line. You could easily keep the truth of your fae heritage to yourself and simply weave the story you wish to tell." Hamish leaned against the galley, tapped the heel of one booted foot in the sand and waited.

"You mean speak a mistruth?"

"I mean you should omit the truth, which you currently do regardless."

"And what of her close ties to the MacDonald? That I cannae allow to continue."

"There is no halting a compeller." He grinned. "She'll be a

handful your mate, but she's still yours all the same."

"I cannae lose her, no matter the secrets I hold."

"Your need to protect her rages just as strongly as her need to protect you does."

"She sails through dangerous waters."

"I take it then 'tis time for us to set sail as well."

"Aye, although I will have a lot of explaining to do with her when I find her. Rally the men."

"'Tis about time you issued that order." With a look of satisfaction, Hamish pushed off the galley, his black leather vest pulled tight across his shoulders and his sword gleaming at his side. He trekked across the beach and yelled to the men, "Extinguish the fire! Our laird wishes to set sail after the lass who's left. We have plenty to do this day, to find her and then to hunt down Gavin MacDonald."

* * * *

With the wind filling the sail, Ella cruised alongside the coastline of Scalpay, the isle almost perfectly round and easily navigated. She searched for any sign of Ethan and Gavin, from the smallest inlet to the wide bays where the forest butted right up to the edge. Finding them was imperative, and preferably before Duncan did too.

As the morning passed and the afternoon wore on, heavy gray cloud swept in across the skies and the waters swelled, the wind whisking through with chilling intensity. Up ahead and set a hundred feet back from the water's edge, smoke curled into the air from the thatched roof of a wattle and daub inn, while a half dozen skiffs sat beached on the pebbly shore before it. She scanned the vessels, although none appeared large enough to hold seven hefty men.

Ropes firm in hand, she turned the sail a touch and with her booted feet braced along one side, crested the waves rolling into shore. She'd seek shelter at the inn for the night. She could do little more this day with the encroaching dark.

As her skiff cruised into shore, she dropped the sail and bounded into the knee-deep waves. With her breeches plastered to her legs, she pulled her boat up onto the curve of the bay and secured it to the closest boulder where it would remain out of reach of any incoming high tide.

The wind blasted through swifter and stronger. Thunder rumbled and lightning speared the sky, a jagged bolt of sizzling yellow. The ever-darkening clouds burst open. Rain pummeled down, pinged off the boulders and slammed into the sand.

Bag in hand, she raced up the broken-shell trail as a lad darted from the inn's side door and bounded over a rail into the corral. He caught the reins of a horse and urged the big black beast inside the stables. The rain beat down harder and drenched, she halted under the protection of the inn's overhanging eaves and dripped water everywhere.

Candlelight danced from behind the latticed windows to one side and the planked front door with its cast iron door knocker, beckoned. She lifted the rapper and knocked.

The front door swung open and a crinkly-eyed man wearing brown trews and suspenders over his cuffed shirt waved her in. "Come inside out of the wet, lass. The wife has mutton stew cooking if ye wish some."

"Thank you." Mutton stew. Her mouth watered and she licked her lips. "The storm hit so fast."

"Aye, storms blow in quickly in these parts. We've travelers aplenty who've sought shelter here this night, so join in the merriness."

"I'm looking for my brother, Ethan Matheson. Might you have seen him?" She stepped inside, stamped the sand from her boots on the thick matting of rushes. "He's been sailing with Gavin MacDonald and his men."

"My wife is the one ye need to ask since she tends to the guests, but I've no' seen any Mathesons or MacDonalds in a good week or two if that's of any help."

"Oh my, the lass is wet through." A flush-faced woman with strands of gray hair trickling free of the knot atop her head, bustled past the man and wiped her hands on the loosely-tied brown apron covering her ample waist. "I'll secure ye a chamber and find ye something dry and warm to wear, lass."

"That would be wonderful. Thank you." She followed the woman up the stairwell leading to the top landing. Doors led off either side of the darkened corridor lit only by the odd candle in an iron wall sconce. At the far end, a young maid of mayhap two and ten swept the floorboards, her brown kirtle too long by an inch and almost tripping her up.

"Lizzie," the matronly woman called. "Did ye change the linens in the burgundy chamber?"

"Aye, Mama."

"Good, lass. Fetch me the lacy blue gown from the spare trunk in my chamber, the matching slippers too, then come and light the fire. Hurry, child." The woman opened a door halfway down the hallway and Ella followed her inside. "This burgundy chamber is all yours, for as long as ye need it. It overlooks the sea and the mainland in the distance." The woman ambled across to a chunky trunk sitting at the end of a large four-poster bed, the burgundy canopy sweeping down to the floor. She pulled out a drying cloth and a clean shift, nodded at her. "I'm Miriam. Do ye wish for aid in undressing?"

"Aye, Miriam, please. I'm Ella, from the House of Clan Matheson." She shrugged off her wet coat and draped it over the wooden rack near the hearth.

"Did I hear ye say to my husband that ye were looking for your brother?" Miriam hunkered down, unlaced and plucked her boots free then propped them to one side.

"Aye, his name is Ethan and he's been sailing with Gavin MacDonald and his men. Seven of them altogether. Have you seen either him or Gavin by chance?" Shivering, she eased her damp cream shirt over her head and laid it over top of her coat.

"I've no' seen those whom you speak of, but I'll keep an eye out and be sure to holler if they arrive. Let me get your breeches for ye." Miriam loosened the ties of her breeches and helped shimmy them down her legs before adding them to the rack. "Being a Matheson, do ye hold the skills of the fae?"

"I'm a compeller."

"Oh, ye dinnae say." Eyes wide, she beamed as she flapped out the drying cloth and wrapped it around her. "Then ye must be the lass we've heard about, the one that's said halted the last battle between the MacDonalds and the MacKenzies at Dunscaith Castle."

"Aye, I did."

"Some dinnae believe the tales told about your clan, but I surely do." Miriam circled her, patted her dry then lifted her dripping hair and rubbed it with the cloth. Done, Miriam slid a shift over her head and the soft white cotton slithered down and brushed the polished floorboards.

Cold air whooshed into the chamber as Lizzie arrived and the lass shut the door behind her, a blue gown in her hands. She handed it to Miriam then knelt at the hearth to light the fire. She pulled husky bark from a log, struck flint with a dirk then once the sparks had caught, laid twigs over top and added a block of peat. The fire crackled and flames sizzled an orange-red hue, an additional welcome heat Ella desperately needed.

"Arms up, if ye will." Miriam lifted the gown to her head and she raised her hands and sighed as Miriam slipped the soft fabric over her then shuffled in behind. Such warmth encased her, the blue velvet swishing to her ankles. Lace edged the sleeves as well as ran down the front and ringed the hem.

At her back, Miriam cinched the bodice in tight and laced the stays then came back around in front and adjusted the low neckline, which sat all scalloped with the sleeves draping half off her shoulders. Never had she worn such a revealing gown that showed so much cleavage before.

"Och, ye look stunning, and the gown is a perfect fit for ye lovely curves." Beaming, Miriam knelt with a pair of matching blue slippers in hand and slipped them on her feet.

"You've been so kind."

"Think naught of it." Miriam opened her dripping satchel and hung her damp clothing from within over the remaining slats in the wooden rack. Her belongings would dry soon enough and she could don her beloved breeches again once they had.

"Take a seat and I'll fix your hair. You've got it into an awful wind-tangled mess." Miriam picked up a brush from the side table.

"I've been out on the water all day." She perched on the chair while Miriam swished in behind her, separated each section of her hair then mindful of the tangles, took care as she brushed out the wet length.

"Lizzie, pop down to the kitchens and bring back a cup of hot tea with a spoonful of honey. Mistress Ella has a raspy voice and the tea will work a treat on it."

"Oh, I'd dearly love that." She almost cried at the thought.

"Right away, Mama." Hands bunched in her aproned skirts, Lizzie hurried out the door.

Ella tipped her slippered feet toward the roaring flames. Out the window, the rain lashed the pane and beyond, the waves crashed in and the skies darkened further as night fell.

She relaxed into Miriam's gentle brush strokes and when Lizzie returned with the promised tea, she sipped the soothing sweetness which trickled down her parched throat and made more tears spring forth. The worry she'd carried for days now pummeled through her, as did her decision to leave Duncan this morning. Mayhap she shouldn't have compelled him, but he'd truly left her with no other choice.

Aye, she wanted her mate, but only if he could be as committed to her as she wished to be with him. Certainly she desired the relationship her parents had been gifted with during their time together, a deep love than no one could ever tear apart.

"Are ye all right?" Miriam patted her shoulder.

"I'm fine." She wiped her tears away.

"Ye are without your brother and have been searching for him. Such a thing can wear a lass down. I certainly wouldnae wish to be without my kin." Miriam set the brush down on the side table and crossed to the door. "Come downstairs once ye've finished your tea. A hot meal awaits and I'll bring ye some bread and stew to fill your belly."

"You've been so kind. You have my immense thanks."

"You're welcome." With a soft smile, Miriam left with Lizzie.

She sipped her tea and once she'd finished the sweet brew, to the very last drop, she rose and walked downstairs, her skirts tickling her legs. It had been a long time since she'd last donned a gown and she fidgeted with the low neckline and tried to lift it a touch, only it budged not one bit.

At the edge of the main room, she halted where the tall screens separated the tables and on her toes, searched amongst the patrons. At the far table underneath the window overlooking the mist-shrouded forest beyond, two warriors sat on the benches with two young women seated between them. In the center of the room, families with small children chatted as they ate.

She stepped closer to the roaring fire and embraced the warmth as it radiated over her. Miriam had left her hair lying loose and long and it blew about her face as the front door opened and the stamping of booted feet resounded toward her.

Two towering warriors shook water from their hooded cloaks, the black folds over their heads hiding their identities from one and all, although there was something about the way the tallest of the two warriors stood that made a shiver chase down her spine. She ducked behind the closest screen and crouched.

"We need to remain on guard while we're here." The tall

warrior slid his gaze about the room, his beady black eyes unmistakable. 'Twas Gavin.

She shuffled a little farther back out of sight.

"If Duncan MacKenzie or any of his warriors arrive, we leave, immediately. I cannae see him giving up his chase, no' after we set fire to Inverarish."

"Aye, Captain. I'll keep a watch out." Hood still pulled low, Gavin's man walked toward the screened table in the darkened corner not far from the front door.

"Gavin, is that ye?" A barmaid flounced toward Gavin, set a tray of tankards down on the corner table and with her lush breasts nearly spilling free from her green kirtle's low neckline, her hips swinging wide, she brushed her chest against Gavin's chest.

"Effie, my sweet. Just the lass I was after." Gavin shoved the wench into the darkened niche under the stairwell.

Giggling, Effie hooked a finger in his belt. "'Tis been far too long since your last visit."

"Aye, and I've a great desire to spend some time with you this night." He grabbed her breasts and squeezed them. "You've a ripe handful here that needs plucking."

"Ye know the way to my chamber."

"Aye, I do." With a leer, he scooped the lass up, tossed her over his shoulder then clomped down the gloomy corridor, one hand sliding under the lass's skirts. He pinched her bottom and Effie giggled anew.

Drat it. She needed to catch Gavin alone if she wished to compel him, that's if her voice remained strong enough to do so. She'd successfully compelled Duncan this morning, so hopefully she'd have no issue with raising a hypnotic tone with Gavin.

The wench's chamber door banged shut and she heaved to her feet, brushed her skirts and snuck down the passageway in their wake.

Outside the lass's door, she gripped the knob as thumping

sounded within. More giggles and a man's deep growl echoed toward her.

"Ella, wait." Ethan stepped out of the shadows behind her, his wet hair plastered to his head and his blue gaze alert. Water dripped from his shirtsleeves and glistened on top of the bits of steel studded within his brown leather vest.

"Ethan, where did you come from?" Gasping, she bounded into his arms and hot tears surged forth. Clinging to him, she whispered raggedly, "I've been searching for you for nigh on a sennight, almost caught up with you on Raasay."

"I knew you'd find me sooner or later. I've been having a difficult time keeping Gavin from causing complete mayhem. Has your chest illness cleared and your voice returned? You're still whispering." He hugged her just as tightly in return.

"I'm on the mend. My voice is still gaining in strength, but this morn, for the first time since I fell ill, I successfully compelled a man and I intend to do so again now, with Gavin, or at least as soon as he tires of the wench.

"I tried to halt Gavin at Inverarish. He certainly would have set fire to far more homes if I had no' been there, although he does no' listen to me, no' one word. I cannae turn him from his current path." He drew her deeper into the shadows of the nook he'd been hiding within, one she'd missed in her hurry to get to Gavin. With a watchful eye, he kept both her and the passageway within his sight. "We need to get Gavin back to Dunscaith and ensure his chief is made aware of all he's done."

"I agree, and I'll aid you however I can."

"Did you sail here alone? I saw our skiff out on the beach and knew to look for you."

"I'm alone, and how did you get past me? I didnae see you come in through the front door."

"I snuck in that way." He gestured farther down the passageway to a side door leading outside, one barely visible in the gloomy dark. "I'm aware Duncan MacKenzie hunts Gavin.

He's been sailing hard on our heels since I infiltrated Gavin's band of men."

"On Raasay, I accepted aid from Duncan, sailed with him last eve until I left him behind this morn. He's most certainly after Gavin, is determined to halt him and make him pay for his strikes against him. I fear with his life as well."

"Why would you accept aid from Duncan?" Her brother frowned and she wasn't surprised.

"I have feelings for him, like that which arise between soul bound mates."

"What?" Shock washed across Ethan's face then the emotion suddenly cleared. "Wait. In truth that actually makes sense. You two had quite the conversation at William's inn and after you told me all about it, I did wonder if mayhap something more lay between the two of you."

"You truly wondered that? You should have said something."

"I could hardly get a word in edgewise. You wouldnae stop rattling on about him the entire journey home. You also seemed fixated on him in the days that followed afore you took ill. You even mumbled his name during your sleep." He crooked a brow. "You awoke me doing so."

"I had no idea."

"If you two are in fact soul bound, then that must mean he holds fae blood."

"Aye, although he denies it."

"I'm sure you can ferret out the truth."

"Try and stop me." She would never give up the desire to learn the complete truth. "I've been waiting three years for him, and now I've finally found him, I dinnae intend on letting him go, or allow him to let me go. Only he needs to learn first just how very deep the bond can run, that no one, no' even a man in denial can truly release the one who holds the other half of his soul. Hopefully he'll come to that realization sooner rather than later."

A crash sounded then the wench's door rattled. Someone thumped heavily against it, again and again. Heavy grunts echoed and with each one, the door shook harder.

"At every inn or village we sail to, Gavin takes one lass after another." Ethan blew out a long breath. "I swear these isles will be riddled with his red-headed ilk afore too long."

A squeal and a lusty groan. The rattling ceased.

"It appears they're done." She squeezed his arm. "We need a solid plan."

"As soon as Gavin comes out, you compel him. We need to get him to Dunscaith Castle where his uncle can deal with him. His attacks against Duncan and the innocent under his command need to halt, although you cannae travel with us back to the MacDonald's stronghold. If you do, it'll raise suspicion amongst his men. Gavin's made his intentions clear. He wishes to leave here once the storm breaks and sail directly to Duncan's land and cause even more mayhem than he currently has. Which means if there's a change in plans, he and his men will presume you had something to do with it."

"Agreed. I can compel him now, then follow at an unnoticeable distance and meet you at Dunscaith." Ethan's plan ran right in line with her own thoughts.

"I give you my word I'll get him there."

"I know you shall."

The door swung open and Gavin emerged and closed the door behind himself. He righted the ties of his brown breeches and shoved the tails of his black tunic in, swung his cloak over his shoulders and tugged the hood back into place.

She stepped out from within the nook, cleared her throat and hoped like hell she could bring her compelling voice forth. "Gavin MacDonald, here me well. You'll leave this inn this night and seek shelter elsewhere from the storm and once all has cleared, you'll continue on to Dunscaith Castle. There you shall account to your chief for your devious actions, both against Duncan MacKenzie and the innocent villagers on Raasay. I will be there to ensure you do. The Chief of MacDonald shall learn of all your misdeeds and no more shall you strike out against the innocent." Her voice cracked on the last word, but his eyes still glazed over. "Am I understood?"

"Aye, seek shelter elsewhere until the storm clears, then continue on to Dunscaith. Account for my actions."

"That likely willnae be enough," she whispered to Ethan, "but 'twill have to do for now."

"You can compel him further once we reach Dunscaith." Ethan kissed the top of her head. "We'll halt his devious actions as best as we can."

"Be careful."

"You too." He gripped Gavin's shoulder and strode with him down the passageway.

The front door banged shut after them and she hurried to the side door Ethan had pointed out earlier and slipped outside. Thunder rumbled and more rain lashed down.

Quickly, before she got too wet, she snuck around to the front and ducked under the protection of the eaves. At the curve of the beach, Ethan, Gavin and his men heaved their vessel into the water, rowed out of the bay then raised their sail. She waited until their boat disappeared into the dark then released a long sigh.

Ethan once again sailed away from her, but 'twas more than necessary this time. He'd been her shadow since her childhood, her closest confidant through the years following Papa's death, and now a man fully grown and prepared to do all he could to prevent blood from being shed. Such pride filled her, would fill Mama as well if she were here. Papa too would have been so proud to see his son becoming the warrior he'd always hoped he would be.

The wind whistled through, swept her skirts against her

legs, the storm wild and only about to grow wilder. Lightning sizzled across the skies and something white flashed near the stables.

"You shouldnae be outside in this weather." A soft voice wisped all about her then the flash of white materialized. Cherub appeared out of the misty dark and took her full form, her white fur hooded cloak flapping back from her shoulders over top of her vivid red gown, her blond hair whipping about.

"Cherub, what are you doing here?" All in her fae village knew her people's guardian. Cherub was an immortal time-walker and the faerie king's daughter, had lived over a thousand years and during that time had aided so many of her fae-blooded kind who walked this Earth, although she was only seen from time to time, and usually always with her mate, Kirk. This night though, Kirk remained nowhere in sight.

"I'm here to ensure you and Duncan are reunited." Her sparkly skin caught the lantern light and reflected it back with such stunning brilliance.

"He's in denial of our bond."

"Then work your wonders on him and ensure he listens to you well. 'Tis time for me to whip up an even fiercer storm that will bring him here and keep him here. Kirk is missing out on all of this fun."

"Where is he?"

"My mate is visiting his brothers at Stirling Castle, although I'll return to him the moment I'm done here and let him know all that's happened." Grinning, Cherub lifted her hands to the air and with a twirl, the wind roared louder and the storm churned into a raging mess. She motioned toward the hefty swell of the sea where a galley's large square sail came into view with one very familiar man standing at the stern.

Duncan's dark war coat studded with steel whipped about his legs and grim anger slashed his face. "He comes." She clutched her chest. "He really comes."

"Aye, your chosen one does and I'll ensure he cannae leave until I deem the time is right. Remember, I'm always here should you have need of me. Simply call out and I'll answer your summons." Cherub blew her a kiss then shimmered away, disappearing just as quickly as she'd come.

"Thank you, Cherub."

Aye, their fae princess always stood so firm beside her people, and now 'twas time for her chosen one to stand firm beside her side. She would do as Cherub had said and challenge her chosen one as never before.

* * * *

Through the cloying dark, the storm worsened and the rain pummeled into Duncan. Finding Ella this night was imperative, and he damn well hoped she no longer sailed these seas but had sought protection from the elements.

Ahead, a secluded bay beckoned with a quaint wattle and daub inn sitting a hundred feet inland, one surrounded by towering pine and elm trees. He'd search this inn for her then continue on should he have no luck. "Lower the sail, and all to oars," he commanded his men.

As they glided into shore, he bounded over the bow, hit the knee-deep waters and surged through the waves. He jogged up the broken-shell pathway toward the front door then slowed at the sight of an ethereal vision appearing out of the dark before him. With her brown hair swaying to her waist and her beautiful eyes fixed on him, Ella stood in a stunning blue gown and he could barely breathe at the renewed sight of her. He'd finally found her. "Are you truly here or just a figment of my imagination?"

"I'm truly here." The velvet of her gown hugged her sensual curves, from the upper swells of her breasts to her cinched waist and flowing hips.

"I've been searching for you all day." Palms planted on the wall either side of her head, he caged her in.

"And now you've found me. It also appears you've arrived just in time to join me for the evening meal." An impish grin lifted her lips. "Unless of course you're chasing another lass, other than me."

"You compelled me, forced me to allow your leaving. You even demanded I see you as naught more than an annoyance until I chose to see the truth and accept it."

"That I did."

"If you ever try to compel me again in such a way, I'll, I'll—" Anger and frustration collided deep within him. All he wanted to do was toss her over his shoulder and cart her to a private room where he could ensure she understood exactly how much he wanted her, only they needed to talk before they ever took that next step. "You're a handful, my grumpy one, but you're still my handful all the same. I cannae lose you."

"What of the secrets you hold?"

"We'll speak of them."

"That sounds promising."

"Your voice also sounds stronger. There's barely any rasp at all."

"I just enjoyed a hot cup of tea with honey and 'twas a most soothing drink." She ran a finger down the front of his chest and molded his damp blue tunic to his skin, her gentle touch searing him like a brand and making fire race across his flesh. "I found Ethan and spoke to him."

"Where? When?"

"Here, and no' long after my arrival. Come inside and we'll speak all about what's happened." She ducked under his arm, opened the front door and walked inside.

He followed her as she weaved around the screened tables holding patrons, the main room lit by a roaring fire and candles flickering atop the tables. In the far darkened corner where little firelight reached, she sat on the bench seat and wriggled along to make more room for him. He eased in next to her, a screen at their back and the two corner walls forming the other two sides of their booth.

Gently, he caught her hand, the long lace-edged sleeves of her gown draping over her wrists as he tangled his fingers with hers. "Last eve," he began, "you lay in my arms without a stitch of clothing on. I want that again this night, to have you in my bed."

"That all depends on our coming conversation. First we need to talk about Ethan and Gavin. I've successfully compelled Gavin. He seeks shelter elsewhere until this storms breaks, then once the weather clears, he'll continue on to Dunscaith Castle where I'll meet him and my brother. Ethan and I will ensure Gavin is stopped, that you'll never come under attack from him again, that his chief ensures it too."

"I'll never allow you to travel to Dunscaith alone. You're my mate." He raised her fingertips to his lips. "Never will you leave me again."

"'Tis quite normal for the males within the bond to worry about their women in such a way, although I know how to look after myself, have done so for a very long time. There is no need to worry about me. Instead, let's clear the air between us. You have secrets you need to share and I wish to hear them this night."

"Trust does no' come easy for me, Ella. I want your word that what I share with you will go no further than us."

"Of course." She gripped his shirtfront, tugged him closer, all rosy-cheeked as she breathed fast. "I've already told Ethan about our bond taking form and he of course guessed you must hold fae blood somewhere in your line, just as I already have. He'll never speak of it to another. You can trust him with your secrets, just as you can trust me."

"None of my men are aware I hold fae blood, other than for Hamish, and that is the way it needs to stay." Through the front door, his men trailed in and a serving maid showed them to their tables. "There's to be no word spoken about our bond with them. Understood?"

"Aye, understood."

"Here we are. Your meal, Mistress Ella." An elderly woman with a loosely tied brown apron covering her ample waist and gray hair coiled into a knot atop her head, set a tray down on the scratched wooden surface. "Mutton stew and fresh bread, and another cup of honey-sweetened tea for ye."

"You're a treasure, Miriam." Ella grinned and accepted the food, picked up a spoon and dunked it into the stew. She moaned as she ate her first mouthful. "Mmm, this is delicious and exactly what I needed."

"Ye voice sounds so much better already." Miriam set a bowl of stew before him. "Welcome to Scalpay, sir. I'll tend to your men as well."

"Aye, please. You have my thanks."

"You're most welcome." Miriam bustled across the room with her tray and disappeared through the side door into the kitchens.

Ella scooped up her bread, dunked it in her stew and took a dainty bite.

He ate his own stew, the richly flavored juices hearty and delicious. "I have an admission," he mumbled as he ate.

"I'm listening."

"In the past, whenever I've met a woman who remotely appealed, I couldnae do more than steal a few kisses afore being overcome with the urge to step away from her." He'd certainly never allowed a lass to touch him, and when he'd approached his brother about the issue, Coll had decreed he'd never been able to tumble a lass proper either, even feared he'd might never be able to.

"Those who are mated can rarely abide the touch of another, no' unless their mated one has chosen willingly to forego their bond, or of course if they've lost their mate due to death. Only then is it possible to move on. I've only ever allowed your touch, will only ever allow it." She set her spoon down, her voice a seductive drawl across his senses, her sweet presence even more so.

"I wish for your touch." All he wanted to do was drown in her heavenly brown eyes, the flecks of gold twinkling so bright.

"Then we should speak, although in private. Move along and allow me out."

He shuffled off the bench, took her hand and aided her to her feet.

"Meet me in my chamber when you're ready. First floor, third door on your right." Her compelling voice swirled so sensually around him, her decree to meet him one he couldn't turn down, not that he wished to.

"I shall be there as soon as I've collected my belongings from my galley." He leaned in and kissed her, licked across her tongue then delved deeper and molded their mouths together until she clutched his arms, her breathing ragged.

"Goodness, I love your kisses."

"I love yours." Rough words, his mind still hazed by the sheer joy of touching her so freely. His men watched on and he reveled in the moment. No longer did he need to hide his desire for her.

"From this day forth, Duncan MacKenzie, you're mine. Never will I forego our bond." Whispered words between them and he cherished each and every one.

"Aye, I'm all yours, as you'll soon be all mine."

Chapter 5

Within the warmth of her chamber, Ella nabbed another block of peat from the wicker basket and tossed it onto the flames while the storm raged outside. The fire sizzled and the flames danced orange and red while the wind rattled the pane. At her back, her chamber door creaked open then clicked shut and she held perfectly still as Duncan's heady scent enveloped her.

"Thank you for the invitation to join you." From behind, he curled one hand around her waist and touched his lips to her ear. "I had the need to change first, didnae mean to take so long."

"You're here now, and that's all that matters." She turned in his arms, slid her hands around his neck and threaded her fingers through his silky black hair. Tingles raced across her fingertips as she leaned into him and stroked the back of his head. He now wore his great plaid belted low at his waist, the tartan slung up and looped over one shoulder where he'd secured it with a silver pin at his chest. She snuggled against him, rested her cheek against his broad chest and snuck her nose into the deep V of his billowy white tunic. "Mated pairs belong together."

"I brought my belongings, have no intention of leaving now I've arrived." He slung his satchel from his shoulder, set it beside the bed then with his hands on her shoulders, turned her around and unlaced her stays.

Eyes closed, she allowed the sensation of his dreamy touch to wash through her, the intimate moment one she only wished to embrace. Aye, he was her mate and there was no other for her, other than him. With the last lacing plucked free, her bodice loosened and the soft fabric slithered down to her feet. In her shift, she stepped out of the pool of velvet, swept it up and tossed it over top of the dressing screen propped in the corner. "I cannae wait to hear how you've come to hold fae blood."

"Unfortunately, 'tis a sad tale." He folded back the bedcovers and gestured for her to slide between the sheets.

"Tell me everything." She eased into bed and tucked the covers back around her while he wandered around to the other side of the bed.

Boots toed off, he laid his wrist and ankle daggers on the nightstand, propped his sword against the headboard then unfastened his kilt and folded it on the corner chair. In naught but his tunic reaching him to mid-thigh, he slid into bed beside her. This moment seemed so incredibly intimate and she smiled as they faced each other on their sides, the light from the fire's flames dancing across his high cheeks. "Are you ready, Ella?"

"More than ready. I'm listening."

"At the age of eight, my brother and I made a pact, to never speak the truth about our birth to another, no' unless we could be assured that the person we told would keep our secret and never use the knowledge against us."

"Your secrets will always be safe with me." The golden strands of their mated bond continued to strengthen and the delicious pull of it drew them ever closer together.

"We're one and the same, my brother and I. Coll has always been right by my side, just as Ethan has always been right by yours."

"I'm glad you have a brother you can trust, just as I trust mine. We need our loved ones to be there for us, exactly as we wish to be there for them in return." She played with the dangling ties of his tunic, loosened the deep V neckline a little more until the smattering of his dark chest hair showed. His skin gleamed in the firelight, his chest so heavily muscled and rippling with strength. "Is it your mother or father who holds fae blood?"

"The only mother I've ever known was Cait MacLennan. She passed away when I was seven. Coll and I loved her deeply. My birth mother, unfortunately, I never knew." He cleared his throat. "To explain I must start at the beginning, to the time afore I was even born."

"Go right ahead." She longed to hear everything, to learn all about him.

"During a time of peace between our clans, a lass by the name of Beth Matheson sailed from the fae village to my father's keep to visit a relative. My father saw Beth and witnessed her fae skill of death-warning arise. Beth received a vision right there in his great hall, sensed death looming for one of his men and immediately hastened to pass the warning along. The man survived, although in allowing my father to see all she could do, she also aroused his greedy desire to hold fae blood within his direct line."

"Colin MacKenzie will take advantage of anyone he possibly can." That she'd learnt well over the years during their warring.

"Aye, and at the time my father was betrothed to the Chief of MacLennan's daughter and upon their marriage was due to receive a large dowry of land, along with the all-important allied relationship he coveted." He spread one palm over her hip and drew gentle circles with his thumb, the pressure so sweet and sublime. "So my father devised a way in order for him to have both Beth and Cait. First, he wooed Beth, spoke handfast vows with her then once she'd conceived, he had her locked away and none permitted entry to care for her, other than a single maid. He intended, once Beth had given birth, to wait out the remainder of the year and a day then wed Cait, only during Beth's captivity she had a vision of death-warning that involved herself and the two sons she carried."

"That is the one thing all those with the death-warning skill fear. Seeing their own death, or that of their loved ones, and being unable to halt what is to come." She pressed her hands to his shoulders, the warmth of his skin soothing her.

"Aye, and after seeing her imminent death, she pleaded with my father to allow Grace, her dear friend from her village, permission to visit her. Grace held the same death-warning skill as Beth and she had hoped that Grace would be able to watch over her, to aid her however she could during her labor and ensure she and her sons lived, only when that time came, she bled so terribly. There was naught Grace could do."

"I'm so sorry." A tear sprang forth and trickled down her cheek.

"I wish my mother had never passed, but afore she did, she asked Grace to watch over her newborn babes and ensure they lived. Grace gave my mother her word she would." He touched his forehead to hers, his voice lowering to a husky whisper. "Following our birth, Coll and I were so sickly, what with being born almost two months too soon, although because of Grace and her dedication to our care, we lived."

"'Tis terrible you lost your mother, although had you perished along with her, I'd be without a mate this day. I'm so grateful she asked Grace to watch over you." Everything within her cried out at the thought of possibly losing him, and before she'd ever met him. Under the covers, she wriggled closer still, rubbed her body against his and sought the comfort she needed. "What happened next?"

"Within days of Beth's death, my father sent for the MacLennan lass and he and Cait spoke vows, her dowry and lands quickly added to his so they might strengthen his own holdings. He then halted Grace's ability to speak of all he'd done. Should Grace have told another the truth about our parentage, then he promised he'd send his warriors to her village and slay as many as he could. He had no desire to lose the lands he'd gained by incurring the MacLennan's wrath and his intentions rang true, a vision assailing Grace should she ever speak the truth to her own kinsmen. So many innocent lives would have been lost."

"Your father is a cruel, hard-hearted man." All were well aware of the Chief of MacKenzie's ruthlessness. "I'd rather never meet him again."

"I'll never permit such a meeting either. My father has deceived even me of late and I no longer trust him, not' that I ever truly have." Brows furrowed, he breathed deep. "When Coll and I were young, Grace returned to her village and Cait continued to care for us, just as wonderfully as any mother could."

"Cait claimed both you and Coll as hers?"

"Aye, although she had little choice. She too fell victim to my father's control. Thankfully though, she did all she could to raise us with all the love our true mother would have." He pressed a kiss to her nose, his warm breath fluttering across her cheeks. "Cait passed the winter Coll and I turned seven, after suffering from an illness which made her breath so ragged she could barely take in any air. I sat at her bedside as she gave up the fight for her life."

"I'm sorry you lost her too."

"She was greatly loved by all within our clan." He cleared his throat. "A year later, Grace returned to us once more after receiving a vision of death-warning regarding Coll and I. When she came to our father's stronghold, she warned us of what she'd seen and that was when we learnt the full truth about our birth, that Cait had no' been our true mother at all. That day we also learnt we'd soon come into our fae battle skill."

"So that's why you hold such strength." She'd witnessed his great ability to battle from Dunscaith's ramparts. "You fought against both the MacDonald and Gavin and held your position well."

"Coll and I both hold the same skill, although afore one and all, our father has always declared our added strength came from holding his strong MacKenzie blood alone."

"Now I understand why you've never harmed a Matheson."

"Aye, for doing so would be the same as bringing harm down upon our own heads. The Mathesons are our blood kin."

"Colin MacKenzie should never have withheld the truth about your true mother and her people from you for so long. In doing so, he took away your right to learn all you needed to know about your fae heritage." She cupped his cheeks, stroked her fingers back and forth over his stubbly jaw. "I'm so sorry you've never had us to stand by your side. We Mathesons do when it comes to each other."

"I have you now, and I wish to claim you as my wife."

"You wish to wed?" Surprise and pure happiness rolled through her.

"Aye, and right this very moment." He gripped the hem of his tunic, lifted it over his head and tossed it behind him where it landed with a soft *swish* on the corner chair.

"Wait. Right now?"

"There is no other way I'll join with you otherwise." He pushed the covers back and she gasped at the sight of his cock rising high and firm from a thatch of black curls at his groin. "Look at me." He caught her face in his hands and steered her gaze back to his. Such a hungry need swirled within his stunning blue eyes. "I wish to accept the bond, to take you as mine, Ella, for us to be man and wife, from this moment forth."

"Aye, please, I want that too." Elbows underneath her, she eased up a touch and gasped as his shaft thickened and lengthened further. It jabbed right into her belly, the head glistening with his essence. "You are the only man I'll ever wish for, ever desire, ever long for. Our clans might no' be at peace, but you and I shall always be so."

"We'll need to speak handfast vows since there isnae a clergyman about." He gripped the hem of her shift, tore a thin strip of white cotton from it then clasped her right hand with his right and wrapped the thin strip around both their wrists. "Will you bind yourself to me as my wife for the next year and a day?"

"For the rest of my life if you'll allow it."

"I want to ravish you senseless." He brushed his lips across hers. "I, Duncan Angus MacKenzie, of Ardan House, pledge my troth to Ella, of the House of Clan Matheson. With this handfast, I take her as my wife for the next year and a day." He hauled her shift over her head, the fabric bunched around their joined hands. Her breasts spilled forth and he lowered his head, licked across one beaded nipple. "Speak your vow now, Ella, afore I lose all control."

With his hot tongue lapping her breast, she murmured, "I, Ella, of the House of Clan Matheson, pledge my troth to Duncan Angus MacKenzie. With this handfast, I take him as my husband for the next year and a day." She unraveled the binding, freed their hands and pushed her shift aside. "You are my stubborn one, and I shall never forsake you."

"'Tis time to seal our vows." Gaze smoldering, he captured her mouth in a scorching kiss, his muscled body a fierce heat she wanted to embrace in every way. "My wife," he murmured as he slid down her body to the end of the bed.

"Duncan, where are you going?"

"I'm allowing my instincts to take over, as I quite often do, and right now they're demanding this of me." He widened her legs and stroked along her inner thighs, his fingers moving all the way to the crease of her groin. Nuzzling her mound, he breathed deep, spread her legs even wider and revealed all of her to his ravenous gaze. With a low rumble, he trailed one finger along her slit. "I want my cock inside you, right here. Compel me, Ella. Make me wait."

"Oh, please, aye." The heat of his breath washing over her made her burn for a full joining.

"I said to compel me to wait, no' to entice me."

"Wait, of course. You must wait." She speared her fingers through his hair and held onto him.

"I've heard my men speak of the pleasure they sometimes take in tasting a lass below, and of having her suck his cock." Blue eyes twinkling, he blew warm air across her lower folds. "Do you wish for me to bring you such pleasure, to taste you right here?"

"You speak so wickedly." She slid her legs along his shoulders, her heartbeat a pounding mess.

"I'll take that as an aye." He grinned and separated her folds. "You're so sweetly pink and all mine." Hands curled around her hips, he lowered his head and swept his tongue across her flesh then delved deeper and licked until a fire blazed in her core and sizzled along her senses. Heat radiated out from where he touched her, made her crazed for so much more.

"Do that again," she whispered, her voice so ragged. Hips lifting, she panted, struggling for breath as a kaleidoscope of emotions surged through her. "I never thought I could be so wanton and make that kind of demand."

"I adore your wantonness." He rose up over top of her, pressed the head of his shaft against her entrance and moaned as he rubbed himself along her slickness. With his hands planted either side of her head, he kissed her, his tongue surging inside her mouth just as she wished for his cock to surge into her below.

"Do it," she murmured, her compelling voice strong. "Make us one."

"You're my wife, always mine." With one hearty thrust, he plunged through her barrier below in one fast and sure stroke, his cock buried so deep within.

She gasped at the fierce intrusion, yet never had she felt so wonderfully full.

"Are you all right?"

"Aye, I'm your wife, your mate, the one who holds the other half of your soul." She caught his face in her hands, brought his mouth back to hers and kissed him, with all the desire and intense need she held deep within her soaring forth. "Move slowly so I might adjust to you."

"I shall, but tell me if I bring you any further pain." Ever so slowly, he slid back out then halted and pushed all the way back inside her again.

She clung to him, the initial pain of his entrance slowly ebbing and when he pushed ever so deeper a second time, a tingle of pleasure radiated out and she sighed at the sheer beauty of it. "More, give me more of that."

"It feels so exquisite being inside of you." He eased out, slid back in and groaned. "Your body is so tight and hot. I want to go deeper still."

"Do as you please." Never could she deny him anything. She stroked over his tight backside, her fingers firm on his flesh as he thrust with an ever-increasing pace that had her crying out for more. Every inch of her channel gripped him. Goodness, she never wanted this moment to end.

"Do you still feel any pain?"

"There is only pleasure now." A heavenly heat roared through her and it sent her mind spinning.

"I need you, Ella." He thrust harder, made her body sizzle and spark and she rocked underneath him, his muscles all hard angles that made her ache at the sheer beauty of him.

His pace increased. So divine. She nibbled along the other side of his neck, rubbed her breasts against his chest to ease the sweet pressure in them. More kisses. She wanted his lips on hers. She kissed him as he slid one hand down between them and stroked over her nub. She wanted to let go, to accept the ultimate pleasure that beckoned and claim it, but not without him. Teetering on the verge, she cried out his name, "Duncan. Do something."

"I cannae hold on any longer." He flicked her clit and she plunged over the edge and soared. Wave after wave of pure bliss rippled through her core and a sizzling array of colors exploded before her eyes in a wicked display. So beautiful.

* * * *

Duncan roared as Ella came, her core pulsing tight around him. No longer could he wait. His seed spurted hot and heavy inside her, his release coming fiercely hard on the tail of hers. Such sensations stormed through him, her hot channel contracting and pulling his cock ever deeper inside her. Shuddering, he gave her every last drop of himself then sated, held onto her as he looked deep into her eyes. "I may form quite the craving for this."

"You took me to a place I've never been afore." She kissed him, so seductively it made his cock twitch and stir back to full life within her.

"'Twas beyond momentous for me too." Never had he experienced such a soul-satisfying joining. He tightened his hold on her, the all-consuming emotions that had taken ahold of him still continuing to thrum strongly. "Are you sore?"

"Possibly, although all I feel right now is a desperate hunger for even more of you." She kissed him again and he kissed her back.

Naught tasted more divine than his woman and he treasured her luscious lips and exquisite kisses. She was so alluring with her soft, creamy skin and brown eyes that sparkled with such effervescence. When he'd joined with her, buried himself so deeply inside her body, he'd lost all control, hadn't had a chance of holding onto it.

"You are somewhat heavy though. Let me up on top for a

moment." She pushed against his shoulders and he rolled onto his back, swept her with him until she came up over top of him.

Slowly, she lifted up until she sat astride his hips, every inch of her body on stunning display as she stretched her hands high above her head and wriggled against his groin, his cock still wedged deep within her and her full breasts swaying so deliciously close.

"Your body is a platter of new treasures I want to taste and devour." Grazing one finger from between her breasts to her belly, he struggled to control his breathing. He swirled through the brown curls covering her entrance and rubbed her nub.

"Oooh, too sensitive." Squirming back, she gasped, her breasts bobbing about.

"Hold still." He tweaked her nipples, the tips so berry-ripe, hard and pointy. He branded this image of her into his very heart and soul, leveraged up farther with his elbows and scraped his teeth across each bud.

"I adore having your mouth on me." Back arched, she pressed those sweet morsels even deeper into his mouth and he soaked in the exquisite moment, wrapped his lips fully around her and suckled until fire raced through his blood and his cock pounded for more.

Unable to halt himself, he lost what remained of his control, flipped her over onto her back, his shaft throbbing, painfully. He plunged into her over and over, her cries for more sending him half-crazed as he took her hard and fast. This bond was more than a gift. 'Twas a connection of the very heart and soul he'd crave for the rest of his days. Aye, never would he relinquish her, not now, not ever.

"Duncan." She seized his butt and pulled him ever deeper inside her. "Make me fly, just as you did afore."

"I would never soar to the heavens without you." He tightened his hold on her, pounded deep and as she raked his back, sheer pleasure coursing across her face, she sent him flying right along with her toward a pinnacle of brilliant white light.

Bellowing, he sank balls-deep inside her, his release so powerful as it crashed through him and she pulsed around him. No more barriers lay between them. They'd been obliterated once and for all. "You're my mate, Ella."

"Aye, and now I'm also one very satisfied mate." She kissed him and cuddled, her eyelashes fluttering down. "A sleepy one too."

"Then rest if you wish." With the heat of the fire moving over them, he slowly pulled out of her, not that he wanted to but the deep need to see to her care had arisen and now wouldn't be abated.

She mewled as he left her but still slumped into sleep. Out of the bed, he eased then crossed to the side table and poured water from the jug into the basin. He splashed his cock then nabbed a cloth from the pile, rubbed a little soap on it and returned to his now peacefully sleeping wife.

Carefully, so as not to wake her, he gently wiped her clean and removed all trace of their joining and once done, settled in beside her, tucked the fur covers over them both and wrapped his woman up in his arms. Oh, how he wanted to shout from the roof tops that she was his chosen one and he'd now claimed her. Never had he known such pure joy and tranquility as this.

She was his everything, his one and all, the greatest gift he could ever have been given.

Aye, he'd accepted the bond and now intended to treasure it.

Chapter 6

Duncan held Ella tight as he awoke to the new day dawning. His heart floated so light and free even though the weather appeared as dismal outside as it had been the night before. Rain slashed down, the skies churning a slate gray, but none of that could alter his immense happiness.

At the core of him, peace and satisfaction reigned. Ella was his, would never belong to anyone else. Aye, and he wanted to wake with her in his arms every morning, to fall asleep with her each night, and to never have her far from his sight.

With her sooty lashes spread across her cheeks dusted with freckles, her breath whispering softly through her parted lips, he wanted only to kiss her. Driven to touch her, he slid his fingers through her long locks, the exquisite mass of brown rippling with lighter shades of gold. Gently, he ran one finger down the creamy expanse of her neck and cupped one full breast. He swished around the globe, her nipple puckering so deliciously. His mouth watered and his cock filled.

He moved to her other breast and swirled around it until that nipple too stood at full attention. Her body was a treasure waiting to be plundered, her soul his and her heart one he would claim too, just as he'd already claimed her body. Aye, his love for her now raged, would never be extinguished.

Over her sides, he stroked, pushed the covers back a touch more and widened her legs. The fire crackled and he swished one hand over her flat belly, trailed his fingers through the thatch of curls and cupped her mound.

She moaned and he crawled farther down the bed, the firelight sending a rivulet of red and gold flickering across her creamy skin. He raised her legs until her bottom lifted off the bed and she lay fully exposed to him. Stroking up her inner thighs, he reveled in the moment before gently parting her folds and easing one finger inside her. With the softest touch, he caressed deep within then dipped his head and licked her. He fondled her nub with his tongue and she moaned again in her sleep and rocked.

"Wake up, my grumpy one," he whispered as he savored her.

"Aye, I'm awake." She blinked her dreamy eyes open, passion flaring strong.

"I intend to wake you in this fashion every morning. That is the only warning you'll get." Stroking harder and faster, he built her pleasure with his fingers and mouth.

"This is such a heady torture, your mouth on me so sweetly intimate. I want to love you as you're loving me." She panted and cupped her own breasts, rolled her nipples between her thumbs and forefingers.

Hell, he needed to taste her there again too, to adore her lush breasts as they deserved to be adored. He rose up, pushed her hands away and fingered one heavenly nipple while he licked the other. Nice and slow, his need to savor the full taste of her overriding all else.

"Mmm, more." She pressed her breasts harder into his mouth and he teased his teeth over one sensitive tip then drew the bud deep inside and tickled it with his tongue.

"Oh, you have one very skilled tongue."

He continued to suck and his efforts won him a soft cry which made his cock harden even further and jab the inside of her thigh.

"Duncan." Body twisting, she seized a breath. "I'm going to come from your mouth on my breasts alone if you dinnae come inside me."

"Aye, come as you please." He ravished her breasts, stroked one finger through her heat below and caressed her.

Gasping, she bucked against him and his balls tightened, his cock trembling with want. She was so slick and close, her needy cries urging him on and he ground his cock into her hip to slow his raging desire, only it didn't ease his need one bit, only hastened it.

"Please, inside me now." She thrashed underneath him, her snug channel tightening around his finger and locking it firmly in place.

"I took you hard last eve and you need time to heal." His balls tightened to the point of pain and a wicked pressure sizzled from the base of his spine around to his groin.

"Oh goodness, I'm healed." She gasped the words then exploded around him and he got lost as her inner muscles clamped down and dragged his finger deep within.

Too lost. He growled, pulled her legs up and spread them wider. In a primitive way he had no control over, he thrust his cock into her in one single hard move and her scream of pleasure echoed off the walls. No mercy. He could allow none now. Over and over, he lunged and she joined him in another wild release that pushed them both to a blinding peak.

* * * *

Limbs heavy and his desire sated, or at least for this moment, Duncan licked across Ella's lower lip as she stretched and curled into him. "Sleep if you wish. We shall remain here until this storm breaks."

"Mmm," she murmured and slowly drifted.

A light tap sounded on the door. "Duncan, 'tis I, Hamish."

"One moment." He popped a kiss on Ella's nose as she snuggled her head deeper into her pillow. Needing to answer the door, he dragged himself from their bed, snagged his kilt and wrapped it around his waist before stepping outside into the gloomy passageway. "This better be important."

In his gray pants and fur jacket, Hamish smiled. "Glad I am to see you've now accepted the bond."

"We spoke handfast vows last eve." He gripped Hamish's shoulder. "I told her the truth about my birth and she's agreed to keep my secrets. Tell my men we've wed, but naught about our bond. 'Twill be as we spoke about yesterday, that I desire her fae blood within my direct line. That is the only reason we've wed."

"Will do. What of her brother and Gavin?"

"She caught up with Ethan on her arrival here." He checked both ends of the darkened passageway, each door remaining firmly closed, the only light penetrating through from a small window at the far end. "She compelled Gavin and he seeks shelter elsewhere from this storm, then once it breaks, he's to continue on to Dunscaith Castle. Ella intends on meeting Ethan and Gavin there, to ensure Gavin is halted in his attacks, that his chief is informed of it all, only I cannae allow her to travel to Dunscaith alone."

"I understand. She's your mate and we can never permit them far from our sight."

"We'll need a plan to ensure all goes well, but we've time to formulate that fully while this storm rages and keeps us landbound."

"Agreed. I'll see to your orders now." Hamish clapped him on the back then with a cheery whistle, strode back down the passageway.

Footsteps echoed up the stairwell and a maid of mayhap two and ten, a flour-smeared apron tied around her waist, passed Hamish on the top step. The lass walked toward him with a breakfast tray in hand. "Mama told me to bring Mistress Ella a tray, to give her a hot cup of tea with honey as well."

"You have my thanks. I'll take this to my wife." There appeared to be plenty for two and he accepted the tray from the lass. "Bring a tub and plenty of hot water as well. My wife will wish to bathe when she awakens." He wished to make certain any soreness from their joining was eased and a bath would certainly aid Ella in her recovery.

"Aye, sir." The lass dashed back downstairs.

He opened the door and slid the tray on the table before shutting it behind him.

Ella stirred and stretched, pushed the bedcovers back and smiled so sensuously at him. "I smell food."

"Come and eat." He pulled out a chair for her.

"I'm famished." She eased out of bed, swiped his white tunic from the corner chair and slid it over her head as she sashayed toward him. The white cotton fluttered past her knees, the deep V neckline dipping all the way to her navel and the sides of her breasts showing. She was such a vision, her dark hair swishing about her tiny waist and her brown eyes flecked with gold, burning bright. She halted before him, her gaze flicking to the window. "The weather looks dismal."

"We'll remain here until this storm breaks." He caught the dangling ties of his tunic and tugged her closer. "I just spoke to Hamish and he'll alert my men of our plans to travel to Dunscaith, as well as inform them of our handfasting. All they are to learn is that I desire your fae blood, wish for it to flow strongly through my own direct line, and now I've ensured that."

"I understand. That certainly is the best option to take if you wish to keep your secrets safe." She rubbed her breasts against his chest, a tease of her pink aureoles showing through the thin white cotton.

"You look beautiful in my tunic." He wrapped one arm around her back, the other around her waist and dipped her backward, the sleeves of his shirt slipping over her shoulders and her breasts bobbing completely free. He buried his nose between both mounds and breathed deep. "Now you hold my name, there is no doubt should the MacDonald learn of it, that you'd become a very valuable pawn in our war."

"You forget my skill." She twined her arms around his neck. "There is none who can successfully capture and contain a compeller. We are very hard to restrain when with only a few words we can so easily see to our own release. I shall also take great care no' to let him hear of our vows being spoken until after my mission is complete. Following that, I simply willnae visit Dunscaith anymore."

"Aye, agreed. You're mine now, Ella, forever mine to protect and care for."

"As you're mine, and I also intend to see to your safety and protection as well during our coming mission. Make no mistake about that." She nipped his ear then so damn hypnotically, murmured, "Release me, Duncan. I wish to break my fast."

"Ella." He growled her name as he tried to wrestle against her compulsion, only he didn't have a chance of doing so. With a snap of his teeth, he straightened and set her back on her feet and let her go.

"Thank you. See, with only a few words I can ensure my own release." Grinning, she pulled the dangling ties of her shirt closed and knotted them, swished across to the table and sat on the chair. She stuck her nose into the steam wafting over the hot cup of tea, daintily picked it up and sipped. Knife and fork in hand, she cut into the bacon and eggs and ate. "Mmm, this is delicious. Come and join me."

He stepped in behind her, slid her hair over one shoulder and sucked the skin of her neck into his mouth and left a nice red mark behind as he did. "You are far more of an appealing meal. I'd rather eat you."

"I cannae provide nourishment, whereas this food can." She

popped a rasher of bacon into his mouth and demanded in her compelling tone, "Sit."

"We need to speak about your commands and when I dinnae wish for you to utter them." He went to sit only a knock sounded and he opened the door and bid the two lads holding a tub between them to enter.

Barefoot and with sooty marks on the rolled hems of their loose-legged tan breeches, they heaved the tub before the crackling fireplace then scuttled out. Maids entered carrying pails of steamy water and filled the tub. Lizzie arrived with clean drying cloths, set them on the side table, added a dash of vanilla scented oil to the bathwater then tossed another log on the fire and once done, bobbed her head and closed the door behind her and the others as they left.

He sat at the table and forked eggs into his mouth, devoured the bacon rashes and smeared a slice of the crusty bread with jam and polished that off as well.

"I need to warn you." Ella watched him as she munched, her gaze firm on him. "You've wed a very strong woman, one who likes to use her skill as needed."

"And you've wed a man who thrives on protecting his loved ones."

"So I see."

* * * *

She couldn't argue that fact, and she had no desire to change it either. They'd work things out in the days to come, ensure both of them survived their current mission.

With the bath beckoning, she rose from the table, hunkered down before the tub, swirled one hand through the water and sighed as a delicious curl of steam wafted from it. "This is the perfect heat. Would you care to join me for a bath?"

"Absolutely." He prowled to the door, slid the bolt home and halted in front of her.

"I want you to undress me." On the tips of her toes, she

kissed his chin, her compelling tone strong.

"That order is one I'll gladly follow."

"I've been without my skill for over a sennight and I crave using it this day."

"I crave you, so provided you dinnae halt my hand as you did afore, then you may compel me all you wish." He lowered to a crouch, his voice a purr as he skimmed his big, warm hands over her calves. Trailing slowly upward, he caressed behind her knees and over her outer thighs, the white cotton of his tunic gliding higher as he rose. Puffing hotly against her skin, he scraped the fabric across her sensitive nipples as he lifted it then tugged it fully over her head and tossed it aside. "There is naught more beautiful to behold than having you standing so unclothed afore me. We need to spend at least a month locked away together, and preferably where no one can interrupt us."

"That I would love. Allow me to undress you now." Sidling against him, she unbelted his kilt and let it drop to the floor in a heap. His cock brushed her belly, hard and hot and she encircled the heavy length with her hand, wanted only to lower to her knees and wrap her mouth around him. "I want to nibble on every inch of your flesh."

Never had she spoken in such a brazen way before, yet standing here with him like this, being so open and honest about her desires, felt so very right.

"I hope this storm never ceases." His gaze consumed every inch of her.

"That would be wonderful." The rain pelted down outside the window, the waves a roaring wash as the surf crashed into shore.

"I need to touch you. 'Tis like a craving in my blood that now released, willnae be halted." He cupped her breasts, eased them together and licked one nipple. The sweetly sensual stroke of his tongue over her sensitive flesh sent a flare of heat rippling straight to her core.

"Mmm, I love how you touch me." Head tipped back and body arched, she soaked in his decadent touch.

"I want my wife." He swirled around the tip with his tongue, sucked her nipple deep into his mouth and she wobbled, her knees buckling until he swept her up then lowered her into the tub.

Warm water cascaded over her flesh, adding more heat to the blaze already burning through her and she wriggled back to make more room for him as he stepped into the tub.

His body was so heavily muscled from hours of sword training, his shoulders so broad and strong and his biceps bulging. As he eased down, his abs rippled, one glorious layer upon layer and each defined contour making her yearn to touch him.

She traced one finger along the delicious tease of black hair narrowing down his unyielding belly where it slowly thickened into a nest of curls at the juncture of his legs. His cock saluted her from the water, the head plump and all hers for the taking. "Our bond grows stronger by the hour."

"Aye, it does." Water sloshed over her chest as he reached over the side of the tub, picked up the soap the maid had left sitting beside it and built a lather between his hands. With a twinkle in his eyes, he lifted her feet and placed them against his chest. "I've always known about the bond your fae kind formed with another, but never could I have imagined it would be like this, that it could rage so strongly.

"This is just the beginning. We have an entire lifetime for our bond to grow even stronger." Smiling, she rested her head back on the rim as he worked the bubbles over her feet. He massaged one of her heels, kneaded along the sensitive arch and around each toe before moving to her other foot and caressing with the same dedicated attention. The water sloshed and her hair swirled over the tops of her breasts.

"I dinnae care to see these hidden from me." He brushed

her hair away, pinched her nipples and grinned as they beaded tight. "It appears you like that."

She more than liked it. A fiery tingle radiated outward from where he'd touched her and she couldn't keep her need contained. "Do that again. Now, harder."

"Aye, my love." He tweaked them again. More pressure this time, just as she'd demanded with her compelling command.

"Perfect. There is naught more seductive than a man who knows how to follow his wife's every request."

He chuckled, stroked over her lower legs then caressed her inner thighs.

She moaned and pushed closer toward him. "Goodness. I cannae think straight when you touch me like this."

"All I wish for you to do is feel." A hungry rumble vibrated from his chest as he plunged one finger deep inside her. He stroked, so hard and fast then curled his finger into a spot that had her gasping with pleasure. She arched, her head dipping back into the water.

Her mind spun in so many different directions, her thoughts almost no longer her own as she bucked, so close to coming. Nay, she wouldn't come without first ensuring he too had experienced pleasure at her hand. Underneath the surface, she searched and skimmed the fiercely hard length of his cock. So big and strong, all of him. She grasped his shaft, one built to send her to the heights of ecstasy. Aye, he was all hers. Swiftly, she pumped him in time with how he stroked into her, each of her moves matching his.

"Ella, that feels so good." He released a low growl, the sound sending a thrill through her. Around the waist, he snagged her, lifted her up then lowered her back down so perfectly on top of him.

Such a flare of sensations ricocheted through her, her channel contracting around him. She rocked over him and he pounded into her then with one thumb, he swirled over her nub until her orgasm built to such a tremendous height she had nowhere to go but over the edge.

"Come for me, Ella. I want to see your pleasure." He flicked her nub and she soared, her core rippling with spasm after spasm of pure bliss, the man before her the only one she would ever desire, with all her heart, body and soul.

* * * *

The moment Ella came, Duncan gave himself over to the sweet pressure of her inner channel sucking so greedily at him and allowed himself his own release. She'd taken him over, every single inch of him and he never wanted it any other way. Kissing her, dipping into the delectable recesses of her mouth, he continued to thrust into her below, her soft moans sending every rational thought from his head.

He grasped her around the waist and lifted her with him as he rose from the tub. How he made it to the bed, he wasn't sure, but when he sank down onto the soft fur covers, 'twas with her underneath him as he cupped her full breasts and lapped at her creamy skin. He gorged himself on both mounds and sucked the pebbled treasures of her nipples deep inside his mouth until she cried out for more.

More, he'd give her. He wanted to make her come, over and over, until she couldn't breathe for the pleasure he gave her. Feasting on her lush flesh, he glided down her body.

"Nay, 'tis my turn." With the sweetest caress, she wrapped her fingers around his shaft, her thumb swiping seductively over the head.

"No' yet." His cock pounded for release yet again.

"Lie beside me, and that's an order." Fiercely compelling words and he gritted his teeth as he was forced to move to do her bidding. Once on his back, she grinned and licked her lips at him. "I do love my skill."

"Your skill is about to drive me insane."

"Aye, but in a very good way I hope." She crawled between

his legs, her breasts falling so deliciously either side of his balls. With her hand sliding around his cock, she peered under her lashes at him. "I'm going to take you in my mouth and have my wicked way with you."

"Have mercy." Fisting the furs either side of him, he held on tight. "Just the thought of what you're about to do has me near ready to come."

"I'll be gentle." In one long teasing stroke, she licked him from root to tip then swirled her tongue over the head.

A blaze of heat built at the base of his spine and buzzed around to his front. "Ella, halt."

"Nay, I've barely begun." Ever so reverently, she cupped his balls and caressed them, then dipped her head once more and settled her luscious pink lips over his shaft and took him deep.

"Ella!" He lifted his hips, his cock hardening with brutal force as she seared him with her sweet mouth. No man could withstand this kind of tortuous loving. He wanted to stop her, yet for the life of him he couldn't. Cradling her head in his hands, he ran his fingers through her hair as she bobbed up and down on him with such exquisite purpose.

"I had no idea you'd taste this delicious. I may no' be able to stop." She sucked harder and he pushed deeper inside her mouth, then got lost as a storm of need whipped around and consumed him. He wanted for her to have all of him, just as he wanted to have all of her.

He gripped her waist, lifted her up onto her knees over top of him then scooted down on his back on the furs and with his head between her thighs, widened her legs and grinned at the treasure of her womanhood before him.

The fire's flickering flames cast a golden-red glow over her pink inner flesh, and that tiny nub where all her pleasure stemmed from, lay awaiting his touch. "Brace yourself, my wife. I intend to devour you."

"I wasnae finished with you yet."

"Dinnae halt me now." With his heartbeat pounding, he sucked the tempting nub into his mouth and lavished attention on her, until she moaned and rocked her hips, whimpered and demanded even more.

Aye, this was the way it should be between them, both needing the other as much as they needed their next breath. He reached up and tweaked her nipples as he sucked on her, the tips so incredibly pink and hard. Onto her back, he flipped her then rose up over top. Fire raced through his blood, his balls tightening and his cock hammering at him. With a roar, he plunged deep inside her hot channel and pumped again and again.

"Kiss me." She captured his mouth with hers and cried out as she came, her inner muscles contracting around him and delivering such sweet pressure.

"There is no other for me, other than you," he growled as he came in a hot rush, every thrust taking him deeper to her core.

"Aye, as there is no other for me either." Her eyelashes drifted down. "Oh goodness, you feel so good inside of me, like I'm no longer missing the last piece of what I've strived to find.

"Aye, we are one, and always will be." He lifted up then slowly pushed all the way back in, ensuring he gave her everything he had to offer. Love her, he would, over and over this day. He wouldn't stop until he'd exhausted them both.

Chapter 7

The next morning Ella wriggled her bottom back more snugly into Duncan's groin where she lay curled on her side in their bed. They'd spent all of yesterday loving each other while the storm had raged outside, then enjoyed an early dinner before devoting the rest of the night to learning everything they could about each other, both of their bodies, hearts and minds.

Now, dawn had arrived and she edged up a little. The fire glowed, the block of peat Duncan had added during the night still burning while beyond her window, gray clouds hazed the sky. At least the rain no longer beat endlessly down. Certainly they could travel this day, could easily set sail soon.

A new level of excitement buzzed through her. Aye, she would need to leave this bed and Duncan's arms, but she'd also be able to continue with her mission and she itched to make everything right, to halt Gavin from any further attacks and to ensure he paid for his misdeeds.

She shuffled around and faced her sleeping mate, traced one finger over the defined cleft in the center of his chin then swished along his jaw, his razz of morning stubble tickling her fingertips. Her chosen one held such rugged appeal, sent her heartbeat racing and her insides into a frenzy of need with merely his presence alone. She rubbed her body against the muscled length of his, the crisp hairs on his chest soothing her achy nipples yet also building her need for even more of his touch so swiftly.

"Is it morning already?" Under the furs, Duncan trailed one warm hand down her back, over her bottom then tucked one of her legs between both of his. He aligned their bodies so perfectly together and she reveled in the moment.

"Aye, and it appears the worst of the storm has now passed. Gavin willnae sit idly by, no' when my compelling command will be gnawing at him. He'll wish to travel to Dunscaith and I need to arrive there first so I can pave the way with the Chief of MacDonald for what is to come."

"I have no intention of allowing you anywhere near the MacDonald without being right by your side. Where you go, I go. Let me just make that clear." With his beautiful blue gaze holding hers, he rocked their hips together.

"You cannae come with me right into the MacDonald's stronghold. Mayhap you can wait somewhere safe and unseen nearby. There are a number of secluded bays where you can make anchor while I go on ahead. No harm will come to me within his walls." She dug her fingers into his shoulders, his biceps rippling.

"I agree to making anchor, but I'll travel with you every step of the way. I can wear a hooded cloak and keep my head down when 'tis time to enter his keep."

"You'll need to do more than keep your head down."

"Then use your skill as needed to keep any and all attention directed away from me, but be assured I willnae be parted from you. You'll no' turn me from this decision." With a firm look, he gave her his drilling stare. "No compelling me otherwise either."

"You are impossible at times."

"Aye, but I'm your impossible." Gently, reverently, he covered her mouth with his and kissed her, his passion held at bay but not the masterful way he always made her feel when they kissed so intimately.

"Duncan?" A rap shook the door. "'Tis I, Hamish."

"I swear he has the worst timing." Growling, Duncan slid out from between the sheets, scooped up the fur from the end of the bed and fastened it around his waist. At the door, he glanced over his shoulder at her. "We'll set sail once we've broken our fast. Agreed?"

"Agreed."

He stepped into the passageway and closed the door after himself

Aye, 'twas time to leave. She eased out of her warm cocoon, picked up her satchel propped against the wall and set it on top of the bed. Flap unbuckled, she pulled out a pair of navy breeches and wriggled them on then fastened the ties at her waist. The loose-sleeved white shirt fluttered over her head and she shrugged on a supple brown rawhide coat, one that would protect her well from the weather since the sky still remained so overcast. Once she'd laced her knee-high black leather boots and strapped her dagger at her wrist, she poured water from the jug into the basin and splashed her face. She cleaned her teeth with a salt and mint paste, combed her hair and wove it into a long plait then searched for something to secure it with. Duncan's white tunic lay snagged on the corner chair, the one he'd worn just afore speaking vows with her. She tugged one dangling tie free and with a soft smile, secured her plait with it.

From the wooden rack near the fire, she collected the remainder of her dried clothing and folded everything away in her bag, left her satchel near the door and gathered up Duncan's scattered belongings. She packed them away in his bag too, but left out a pair of pants, tunic and a jerkin for him to change into.

"Hamish is informing the men of our coming departure." Bare-chested, the fur barely hanging onto his hips, he returned with a tray in hand and knocked the door shut with his hip. "One of the maids brought us our morning meal."

"Wonderful. I'm famished." She took the tray from him and set it on the side table. "Dress if you wish."

"I've also given Hamish orders to ensure none of my men wear our clan tartan while we sail along Skye's coastline. The banner at the center mast is to be taken down as well. We'll travel with all stealth this day." He sauntered to the bed, let the fur drop and gave her a tantalizing view of his firm buttocks, although all too soon he drew his black leather pants and tunic on, slipped his padded jerkin over his shoulders and fastened it at the front. Sword belted at his hip, he hid other various weapons around his body, those that every battle-hardened warrior wore.

"I'm relieved all precaution will be taken."

"I'd rather we had no need to travel to Dunscaith, particularly since my last journey there didnae go so well." He scrubbed a hand across his bristly jaw, crossed to the basin, dipped a cloth into the water and wet his jaw. With one brow arched at her, he said, "Yet had that battle never occurred, I wouldnae have met you, and that moment I'd never take back."

"Nor I either. Allow me to shave you." She joined him, pushed his shoulders until he eased down and perched on the edge of the table. Nudging his legs apart, she nestled in between them and picked up the bar of soap.

"No woman has ever shaved me afore." He settled his hands on her hips, the black leather of his pants molding his strong thighs.

"I should hope not." She snuggled deeper into the V and he smoothed around to her backside.

"I would trust no other with a blade so close to my neck."

"Your trust is appreciated." Giggling, she built a lather with the soap and smeared it across his sharp black stubble, slid her dirk free from her wrist sheath and turning his cheek with one finger, held the blade nice and close to his skin.

"You hold so many skills, and it appears shaving is amongst

them. Is there aught else you can do which you've yet to tell me about?" Back and forth, he caressed her bottom, the bulge in his pants growing thicker and longer.

"I can climb trees with ease." She ran the blade in a smooth line down, from his ear to his chin. "Scale cliffs too. My grandpa taught me and Ethan."

"Well, no more tree or cliff climbing for you, no' unless I too am there."

"Even though we've wed, I willnae allow you to mollycoddle me." She ran the blade right under his nose, tapped his jaw shut before he could answer her back then lifted his chin with one finger and slid the blade down his neck in long and even strokes. Once done, with not a whisker remaining, she dabbed his skin with the cloth, cleared the last of the suds away and sheathed her dagger.

"I'll ensure your protection as I see fit, Ella."

"As I'll ensure yours." Leaning into him, she murmured, "I've never needed someone to catch me when I fall."

He slid one hand around the back of her head, his fingers sliding through her hair. "Now we've completed the bond, if you fall, I fall."

"Then I will simply take all care to never fall." She dotted kisses over his nose and cheeks. "Mmm, now your skin is all smooth and unable to abrade mine."

"If you ever need me to shave, simply ask and it shall be done. 'Tis time I fed you." He eased up, caught her elbow and guided her to the table and their waiting meal.

Once she was seated, she sipped her tea sweetened with honey. "I shall miss this place. Miriam anticipates my every need."

"I'll bring you back, as often as I can." Across from her, he slid his dagger free, sliced the crusty bread then stabbed some of the bacon and egg and layered it on top of the slices. He handed one slice to her and munched on his own slice before raising his tankard to his mouth and gulping down the warm cider.

"Load the galley with enough provisions for our coming journey!" Hamish's bellow echoed through the window from outside.

"We need to hustle." Duncan polished off the last of the bacon and egg, pushed his chair back and collected their bags.

With her meal finished too, she tucked her chair in and slipped out the door with him.

In silence, they trod downstairs and walked through the front door. Ahead, Duncan's warriors swarmed the shoreline and she halted on the pebbly sand where the surf rolled in. Breathing deep, she took in Scotland's freshest air as it whipped around her. The sea surged and swelled, the wind whistling through and tugging strands free from her plait and sweeping them across her cheeks. Across the waterway, her village lay nestled along the mainland, the craggy hills and grassy moors of the Highlands rising high and spreading wide beyond it.

To the south, the Isle of Skye beckoned. Ethan was so close. Hand to her brow, she took in the familiar curve of the coastline rounding the northern tip of Sleat. The gray clouds in that direction thickened further, and a squall out at sea sent rain sleeting down along the length of Kyle Rhea. "That does no' look promising."

"Mayhap that squall will blow itself away by the time we reach the kyle." Duncan swept her up in his arms and carried her through the knee deep waves then lifted her over the side of his galley and bounded in behind her. At the bow before his men, he dipped her backward, kissed her cheeks and nose then set her back on her feet.

"Are you staking your claim?" She rubbed up against him, happy to stake her own claim as well. "Because you missed my mouth by an inch if you were."

"If I kissed you proper right now, then I'd never stop." He slipped his hand around her elbow and guided her down the center aisle to the stern, tucked their bags underneath the rear bench seat and called out, "We sail for Skye, will make berth at a secluded bay near Dunscaith where we'll no' be spotted. All to oars. We leave with all haste."

His men were far more heavily armed than she'd ever seen them before. They carried swords, battle-axes, and bows and arrows strapped to their sides and backs as they took their positions on the benches and rowed their galley clear of the bay.

"Hoist the sail." Duncan adjusted the rudder and as they cruised the waters toward Skye, the white-capped waves rose higher and pitched them about.

She searched the rocky beaches bordered by high cliffs for any vessels similar in size to Gavin's. While she did, Hamish too kept a lookout for the same from his position at the bow.

Nothing. No sign of Gavin. She wrung her hands together. There were plenty of other lodgings farther along the main sea route toward Dunscaith, taverns and inns aplenty where Ethan and Gavin could've found safe harbor. She'd keep searching.

As the waves heaved higher and the wind blew stronger, she slid about on the bench and struggled to remain in place.

"I've got you." Duncan lifted her off the seat and set her in his lap, banded one arm tight about her waist and kept her seated in place. "Dinnae fret, love. Well find them, or meet up with them at Dunscaith."

"That is what I fret about." What if she shouldn't have let Ethan leave with Gavin on his own at all? Aye, if she'd gone with Ethan, Gavin and his men would certainly have been suspicious of her decision to join them, particularly when 'twas well known she sought peace over any blood being shed. "I cannae help but second-guess my decision in allowing Ethan to leave without me."

"He's your brother. We're all overprotective of our loved ones."

"Even as strong as he is with the battle skill, mistakes can still happen." She nibbled on her lower lip. "I'm also leading you and your men into danger." That danger growing by the minute as they traversed the waterways closer toward the MacDonald's stronghold.

"There isnae a day that passes when danger does no' follow me around." He scanned the seas ahead, the choppy waves slapping into the bow as they rode the ever-rising swell toward the thin channel.

"This storm has no' passed at all."

"Aye, the squall grows stronger."

The wind rushed all around and battered the sail. Waves crashed over the side of the galley, waters sloshing across the deck and making it dangerously slick. Several men grabbed pails and scooped the wash back over the side.

"We're also about to hit the crosswinds at the eastern tip of Skye." He shoved to his feet, set her back on the bench. "Stay right here while I navigate our way around the headland."

"Be careful." She squeezed his hand. "If you get hurt, I willnae be happy."

"Duly noted, my grumpy one." He tightened the ties of her brown rawhide coat then marched up the aisle. With the sail's ropes in hand, he kept one and tossed the other to Hamish. The two of them bounded up onto the side of the boat and braced their feet wide, the ropes twined around their arms and their gazes narrowed on the heaving swell and fierce gale.

The crosswind slammed into them, so hefty and fast, the massive square sail pulled agonizingly taut. The gale sent the galley shooting off like an arrow and she careened along the bench and banged into the side.

Another howling blast hit hard on the heels of the first and their galley rose half out of the water on Duncan and Hamish's side. Both countered the move, leaning farther back, the two men half out over the water while Duncan's warriors heaved closer to them and balanced the weight.

They picked up even more speed and skimmed the high waves, while up ahead the high cliffs of Skye rose and the rocky shoreline swelled out into the sea. Waves crashed over black boulders and sprayed high. She needed to find something to secure herself to this seat with, and before they entered the kyle.

Duncan heaved on the ropes and thunder boomed.

Torrential rain slashed at her, stung her nose and cheeks and drenched her through. She heaved to her feet then tumbled over and clawed for a hold on the slick boards of the hull.

"Ella!" Duncan's biceps bulged as he held the ropes firm and controlled the power of the wind he'd harnessed in the sail. "Slide under the seat. Now." His voice got half-whipped away on the wind.

The last thing she wished to do was lose sight of him, but get under the seat she would. She scuttled toward the bench but the galley crested a massive wave and she skidded away.

"I've got you, my lady." Ivor plucked her from the planks, his arms firm around her as he kept her from sliding any further, his legs as thick as tree trunks and his body immovable.

"Thank—watch out." A huge wave loomed and they sailed toward the peak, the bow pitching sharply upward then slamming back down as they soared over it. The sheer force of it tore her from Ivor's arms and she went flying, right over the side and into the waves.

She hit hard and went down.

Her head shattered with pain, the turbulent waters surging and dragging her ever deeper. The rushing current tossed her about, so deep within the cloying dark and she kicked with all her might and tried to fight the fierce underwater rip. She got churned all about, couldn't tell which way was up or down anymore. Nay, she had to keep a clear head before she ran out of air. Never would she allow the sea to take her, not now she'd finally found her chosen one and he'd claimed her, and certainly not when Ethan needed her so desperately. Mama too would never survive her death. Papa's had been hard enough on them all.

She brushed against something and lurched around. Ivor appeared within the murky dark, cinched an arm around her waist and firmed his hold on her. Such piercing green eyes, his pale hair swishing about his face.

He pointed upward and kicked, heaved them both through the twisting current and in a burst of bubbles, they broke the surface as gushing waves slapped over them. "Are you all right?" he yelled over the might of the storm.

"I am now you're here." More waves dumped over them and she struggled to stay afloat. Gulping great drafts of chilly, foggy air, she searched through the pelting rain and fog. "I can barely see a few feet in front of me. Where's the galley?"

"Well gone now. I'll get us to land." Ivor stuck one hand in the air, caught the position of the wind. "This way."

"Ella!" Duncan's shout blasted from somewhere up ahead.

"Duncan!" She screamed his name as waves tumbled them about. He had to have jumped overboard.

"We're here," Ivor yelled.

"I'm coming." His shout was closer, and then he was there, emerging through the sleet and rain, bobbing overtop of the high swell. Growling low and deadly, he snatched her from Ivor and hauled her fully up against him. "You were supposed to slide under the bench. That damn rogue wave sent you flying."

"Ivor found me when I couldnae kick back to the surface." She wrapped her arms around his neck.

"My laird." Ivor jabbed a hand in the direction they needed to go. "I can just make out the cliffs of Skye and a bay."

"Aye, we'll head there." Duncan held her tight and heaving deep breaths, propelled them both through the whitecaps. A bird squawked as it soared somewhere overhead and the surf rolled them into shore.

As her feet scraped the sandy seafloor, she tried to stand,

only her legs wobbled and—

"I'll carry you." Duncan swept her up in his arms, slogged up onto the beach then collapsed onto his back with her sprawled over top of him, the sand wet and mushy underneath them and the rain pelting endlessly down.

Ivor stumbled in after them, his leather pants plastered to his legs and his war coat drenched. He flopped down onto his back next to them, his exhaustion clearly as complete as theirs.

"I owe you my thanks." Duncan eyed Ivor. "For saving my wife. I'll ensure you're well rewarded for what you've done this day."

"Nay, my laird, there's no need for a reward." Ivor heaved up into a sitting position, water dripping from his hair. Such torment flashed in his eyes as he slid his gaze to her. "I apologize, my lady."

"For what exactly?"

"I have a confession. I first believed you to be our enemy, couldnae understand why my laird would bring you on board following the fires at Inverarish. You hold the skill to compel, commanded us during the battle at Dunscaith and sent us fleeing. Even though you claimed to have no voice, I still feared you'd use your ability against us. At any time, you could have sent us all to our deaths, and with naught but a single word. I ask for your forgiveness. I was the one who tossed you overboard, and never have I regretted a decision more."

"I would never harm anyone, Ivor."

"Aye, I'm aware of that now."

"You're the one who tried to kill my woman?" Duncan gritted his teeth and pinned her behind him as he shoved to his feet, his low and deadly tone sending shards of ice skittering down Ella's spine.

"I am, and acted wrongly, very wrongly." Ivor stood, withdrew his sword and handed it hilt first to Duncan. "Seek the punishment you please." He slowly lowered to one knee, head bent.

"Nay." She pushed past Duncan and gripped Ivor's hands. "You just saved my life and I willnae see it lost right here on this beach. So many fear my skill, Ivor. You arenae alone in that regard, but once people come to know me, they soon learn I would never bring any harm down upon another's head, no' even that of my enemy. I forgive you, Ivor." Holding her breath, she snuck a look at Duncan over her shoulder. Fury slashed his face, his hand fisted around the sword hilt. He wanted to kill Ivor, but she couldn't allow it. She faced the man who'd made a bad decision and had no need to pay with it with his very life. "You made a deadly mistake that night, but from this moment forth you will never judge another so unwisely. I want your word that you'll never attempt to harm me again."

"Aye, my lady, I would never lay a hand upon you, no' now, no' ever again. My laird has taken you to wife and my service extends to you, but more than that, I've seen your true nature and will gladly do all you've asked of me. Unfortunately, though, my punishment is still necessary."

"Since 'tis me you harmed, then it should be me who decides your punishment." She needed to show Duncan how very much she needed Ivor to remain alive, which meant she had only one choice. "I will hear your oath of protection. I wish for you to be my personal guard during this mission."

"Pardon?" Something flickered within his green eyes— hope? He glanced over her head at Duncan and that hope flickered straight away.

"Ivor, I shall no' be an easy mistress to protect. I can be feisty and stubborn, and at times I can act without thought for my own welfare. You'll be hard-pressed to keep me out of trouble, but I believe you're the most suitable for the position."

"I would be honored to give you my oath." He dipped his head toward her. "My lady, I give you my vow of protection. Never will I allow another to set a hand upon you with the intention of doing you harm. I will be your servant, from now until the end of my days. Will you accept my oath?"

"I will." She squeezed his fingers. "Rise, Ivor. I already have a request of you."

"Speak and 'twill be done." He stood, firm resolution in his gaze.

"I am freezing cold and have no wish to remain this way." She held out her hand to Duncan for Ivor's sword. "My guardsman will require that."

"I would rather still have his head." Through gritted teeth, Duncan snarled at her as he handed it across.

"Thank you." She handed Ivor his sword, shivered and rubbed her chilled arms. A hundred-foot high cliff curved around the bay, the odd clump of scrub protruding from the cracks. A cliff that appeared very familiar. "Oh my. I know this place."

"You do?" Duncan wrapped his arms around her from behind and tried to buffer her from the fierce wind and rain. "How exactly?"

"My grandpa brought my brother and I here to scale this cliff. Three and ten I was at the time, Ethan eight. Grandpa harnessed a rope around my waist then secured it to the lone pine tree towering at the top. Both Ethan and I descended then climbed back up. 'Twas such fun."

Duncan frowned at her.

"Of course that had been on a fine day, the cliff's hand and footholds easy to find and no' slick with the rain as the sheer rock is this day. As far as I can recall though, this cliff is the only way in and out of this secluded cove."

"There is no need for us to leave this place. Hamish will return and we'll hail him when he does."

"Might we explore this bay and see what we can discover until then? When Grandpa brought Ethan and I here, he told us of a cave which sat somewhere along this bay, one that held a pool of hot water, only we never did find the entrance to it that day. We should look for it now. A warm pool would be heavenly to discover right about now."

"If there is a hidden cave nearby with such a pool of hot water, then I'll find it." Ivor sheathed his blade and eyed the massive rocks jutting out either side of the thin stretch of sand. He stalked toward the cliff face and began his search. Sweeping methodically along the rock wall, he patted and pulled out tuffs of scrub as he searched for the hidden entrance.

"When I saw you flying over the side of the galley"—Duncan turned her by the shoulders to face him—"my heart nearly catapulted from my chest. I barely had time to toss the ropes to one of my men afore I dove in after you and Ivor."

"I couldnae allow you to punish him, no' when he had just saved my life."

"He is fortunate to have received your forgiveness. I can accept your request for him to be your personal guard since he dived in after you, found you and kept you safe until I arrived, but I'll be watching over you as well."

"Thank you." She hugged him, his strong embrace soothing her deep within.

"Let's aid Ivor in finding this cave, if there is one."

"Grandpa never speaks a mistruth. 'Tis just a matter of us finding the entrance." She walked across to the cliff face, palmed the slick, craggy stone wall and surveyed the surface rising high. Several hand and footholds lay within easy reach and offered a variety of paths leading upward that one could scale. At the halfway point, a short ledge ran in a diagonal line all the way to the top, so once one made it that far they could safely shuffle up the ledge then over the top lip. A far safer option that slogging back into the storm-tossed sea and swimming to the next cove, that's if Hamish didn't find them soon.

"I believe I've found the entrance." Ivor heaved a thick clump of bush away from the wall. Dirt and stones poured down on him from a crack in the rock above his head, although he continued on.

"I'll aid you." Duncan marched across and cleared the scrub from one side until the two of them had unplugged half of the crevice.

"Aye, this is most definitely an entrance to a cave." She scrambled in between them and clawed at the dirt and brushwood still wedged within the parting in the rock wall.

"Nay, out of the way, my lady. There's no need for you to dirty your hands." Ivor lifted her up and swung her in behind him.

"I want to help." She tried to wriggle back in but with one extremely stern expression from Ivor, she huffed and instead stayed right where she was. "You're so mean."

With a chuckle, Duncan slapped Ivor on the back. "You and I are going to get along rather well if you continue to master that look on her. I could use the aid in ensuring her protection."

"Excuse me, but you two can just stop acting so very chummy right now." Yet she couldn't help but smile at the return of their camaraderie. As they cleared the last of the scrub and dirt away, they revealed an entrance that deepened into the rocks through a long passageway and she jiggled about as the rain thankfully began to ease into a drizzle. Wonderful. Nature was now granting them some leeway. "I cannae wait to tell Grandpa and Grandma about this cave. They'll both wish to visit this place too."

"Where do your grandparents live?"

"Here on Skye. They have ever since I was a wee bairn, nearer to Kinloch harbor, only a day's ride from Dunscaith."

"Not at your village on the mainland?"

"Nay, but they are only a few hours' sail away." She grinned wide. "I cannae wait for you to meet them, Mama too. She resides at the village with Ethan and I."

"Then let's pray there's a pool of hot water within as your grandpa told you, so we might share that news with them all when I meet them."

"There'll be a pool. I've no doubt of that."

"I'll go in first, ensure all is well." Ivor wedged himself sideways and scraped through the narrow opening. Over his shoulder, he called back, "I willnae be long."

He disappeared into the darkened recesses of the passageway while behind her, the surf crashed in and the rain eased even further, although the fog remained thick and heavy, appeared set to stay for quite some time.

Ivor returned, emerging out of the darkened recesses with his green eyes bright. "All is clear and there is indeed a pool of hot water. Steam plumes from it." He dipped his head in reverence to her. "I wish for my lady to warm herself well. I'll wait outside for Hamish's return. I cannae have him sail right by and miss us."

"Thank you, Ivor." She reached up on her toes and kissed his cheek. "Stand where you willnae get a chill though, and that's an order."

"Aye, my lady." Red suffused his cheeks and he ducked his head as he shuffled past her and took his position outside at the entrance.

"Come with me." Duncan steered her down the gloomy tunnel and halted at the end.

Within the cavern that opened up before them, water lapped onto a small curved beach of grainy white sand, the pool surrounded by massive black rocks. Steam swirled and drifted out a thin vent in the craggy ceiling high above while a trickle of light streamed through and speckled over the pool's glassy surface.

"This place is so beautiful." No waiting. Beyond eager to get into the hot water, she kicked off her riding boots and draped her brown leather coat over the closest rock.

"Here, let me aid you." Duncan loosened the ties of her breeches, tugged the cloying, wet fabric down her legs and laid them over top of her coat. "Leave your shirt on."

"Are you coming in with me?"

"Of course." He toed off his boots, removed his weapons and jerkin then in his leather pants and tunic, scooped her up and walked into the pool with her. Deliciously warm water washed over her as he surged through to chest depth. Gently, he set her down on her feet on the sandy base and nodded. "Go down. Warm yourself through."

"This is glorious." Eyes closed, she sank and blessedly warm water closed in over her head. Heat washed through her, eased the chill from her skin and once she thrust back to the surface, she pushed her wet hair from her face and grinned. "Your turn."

"Only with you." He caught her hands, draped them around his neck and dived with her. Down they went, the water swishing all about, his arms banded tight around her waist and their bodies locked together.

Such relief burst through her and she captured her chosen one's face in her hands while they swam deep within the pool's depths. A more peaceful moment she'd never known.

* * * *

Holding his woman safe and secure in his arms filled Duncan with such relief. He kissed her, right under the water, molded his mouth to hers and embraced the sheer magnitude of his love for her. Aye, he'd fallen so swiftly for his compeller who loved so greatly, would gladly be her slave for the rest of his days.

To the surface, he pushed them and emerged with the sweet curves of her bottom firm in his hands and unable to hold back, kissed her again. "I love you, Ella."

"I love you too, with more love than my heart can hold at present." She played with the opening of his tunic, loosened the ties a little more. "I also cannae help but think that our arrival here, no matter how dangerously it came about, was meant to be."

"Aye, Hamish would surely have been forewarned about this. I cannae see how it could all have passed him by." Although never would he allow her life to be placed in such danger again, only how to ensure that, he'd need to consider.

Pushing through the water with her in his arms, he made the ledge rimming one side and lifted her onto it, her white shirt bunched over her lap and her long legs on exquisite display. Gently, he eased his hands in under the hem and palms flush against her warm flesh, stroked higher, the wet fabric sliding over the backs of his hands like sheer silk.

With a catch to her breath, she spread her legs wider and he snuck in between them and continued exposing her body to his greedy gaze, inch by incredible inch. She had the most enticing limbs, sweetly curved calves and lithe thighs, all leading to an apex where a thatch of brown curls covered her womanhood.

Breathing deep, he took in her honeyed scent and rolled around in heaven. Everything about her called to him, from her beautiful body and free spirit, to her fierce determination and intense love for all those around her. Certainly if he ever lost her, he'd never survive it. Her safety must always come first.

"What are you thinking?" She swayed back, hands braced on the ledge either side of her and her back pressed against the rock wall.

"Of how I need to ensure your safety." He stroked her cheeks, caught her mouth with his and sucked her tongue between his lips.

"I'm safe now, and that's all that matters." She kissed him back, so greedily, just as greedily as he kissed her in return.

He moaned into her mouth, his cock hardening something fierce and pulsing with a throb from base to tip that warned he'd best pull back or else he'd take her right here in this place. That he couldn't do, not when Ivor might walk in on them at any moment. 'Twas damn inconvenient having his man so close.

Easing back a touch, he tried to retreat only she gripped his shoulders and kept him pinned in front of her. "You're no' leaving me now. Make love to me."

"I shouldnae." Except all rational thought fled his mind and his body deceived him. Hands pushing her shirt higher and his head lowering to her creamy inner thighs, he whispered against her flesh, "I vow to always keep you safe, Ella. Never will I place your life in danger again."

Chapter 8

Ella wanted Duncan with a desperate desire that couldn't be halted. She lifted her shirt over her head and dropped it onto the ledge beside her, the need to join with her mate far more necessary than aught else. Almost perishing at sea had frightened her, but joining together would help ease some of that fear. "I never want to live on this Earth without you."

"Or I without you, although right now I should step away. Ivor remains so close, and Hamish could return at any moment." He shook his head as if trying to clear it, then growled and eased her breasts together. With one swipe, he licked across her sensitive nipples and sent a bolt of pure pleasure coursing straight to her core.

Liquid heat invaded her, made her long to have him deep inside her, right now, without another moment's hesitation. She arched her back, thrust her breasts out farther then whimpered when he latched onto one tip and suckled her nipple deep. He had the cleverest tongue and mouth. "Make me yours, Duncan."

"We need to stop." He gripped her hips, lifted her from the ledge and into his arms, the water swishing across his tunic-covered chest.

"Nay, there is no stopping this joining. We need each

other." Under the surface, she fumbled to find the ties of his black leather pants, managed to snag and tug them free then released his cock. It throbbed heavy and hard in her hand and with her legs hooked around his waist, she guided him to her entrance. "Come inside me."

"If I do, I'm no' sure how long I can hold on." With a fierce growl, he thrust deep.

"Oh, perfect." Head tipped back, she moaned her pleasure. So sublime, and as he lifted her up and dropped her back down over top of him, she moaned again. The depth of their bond had caught her within its spell and never would it release its heavenly hold on her. Aye, their souls had connected that first day they'd met and no matter how far they ever traveled from each other, they would always long for this joining and holding each other close.

Reaching underneath her, she gently cupped his balls with one hand while he pumped into her harder and faster. Ravenous sensations stormed through her, until she could no longer hold on. Letting go, she gave herself fully over to her mate and with her thoughts scattering, flew toward the heavens, her release exploding violently along with his as he pounded into her, his seed spurting straight from him and deep into her core.

"Ella?"

"I'm right here." She touched her forehead to his as he eased his thrusting.

"I'm going to take you back to Ardan House. You'll be safe there."

"Pardon?"

"You almost drowned and if I ever lose you, I too would wish for a fast death so I might join you beyond the veil."

"'Tis I who must complete this mission, find my brother and ensure Gavin is dealt with so he can no longer continue to hound you or those under your care. He must answer for his actions."

"I agree, but I'm your husband and my word will stand. Your fall into the sea was a warning, one I must heed. You'll be far safer at Ardan House than here on Skye." He slid free of her, set her feet gently down on the sandy base, the water swishing about his chest as he righted his pants. From the ledge, he snatched her white shirt and tugged it over her head before pushing her arms through the clingy, wet sleeves. "I'll find Gavin and deal with him."

"Nay, you cannae think I will abide by your decision to suddenly alter my mission. I'm perfectly fine and will remain so." How dare he try and use what happened this day against her. Anger flushed through her and she surged out of the water, plucked her navy breeches from the rock and hopping from foot to foot, managed to haul them up. Once she'd fastened them at her waist, she stuffed her feet into her riding boots and strapped on her wrist dagger, wrung the water from her brown coat and donned the supple leather, still slick and wet but it'd have to do.

"I'm your husband, and my final word stands." Water sluiced down his black leather pants as he pulled his jerkin on over his dripping black tunic. He strapped his weapons in place and stuffed his feet into his boots.

"Your worry rages and I understand that, but—"

"No arguments." He shoved a hand over her mouth and gritted, "I cannae lose you, and right now I might be acting on my emotions but those have never failed me afore. You're going to return to Ardan House where I know you'll be safe. There I'll leave you, while I return to Skye."

She pushed his hand away. "I willnae allow you to force me to your will. 'Tis my duty to care for my loved ones, and leaving Ethan to deal with Gavin on his own is unacceptable."

"I will watch over Ethan for you." His unyielding expression said he wouldn't back down, not on this issue, not now.

Neither would she.

"Listen to me well, Duncan MacKenzie." She cleared her throat and allowed her compelling voice to rise. Never would she hand this all-important mission over to him, not when doing so would be sending him directly to his enemy's doorstep and into an even greater war. He was her soul bound mate, hers to protect, always and forever. "You will do exactly as I say. No moving, no' one inch. You will be as stone, unable to chase me as I leave, unable to speak as well. Am. I. Understood?"

* * * *

Damn it. His woman wasn't going to get away with this. Never would he allow her to compel him and place her very life in danger by doing so. He tried to grab her, to halt her however he could, only he hit the ground. Stiff and unmoving, he lay there on his back, breath ragged and his mind screaming at him to move, to make chase as she dashed out of the cavern and disappeared from his sight.

His fear for her gripped his heart like a fist and twisted hard.

Fighting with every breath he had, he shoved and heaved against the rigidness of his stiff muscles. Even his voice remained mute, his lips stuck together by the command she'd issued.

Long minutes passed, mayhap an hour and there was naught he could do about it. Never had fear struck him so hard. If anything should happen to her because of his inability to keep her safe, hell, even he'd happily slice his own head from his shoulders.

"My laird?" Ivor's voice rang in his ears and his man bounded in beside him, grabbed his shoulders and heaved him to his feet. "Hamish has returned and the men await us on the beach. Why are you so stiff, and where is my lady?"

"Ella compelled me," he finally managed to push through tight lips. "Keep jostling me about. 'Tis aiding me in loosening up."

"Ella didnae pass me by. That I give you my word on." Ivor jerked him back and forth and more of his stiffness eased, his voice as well.

"Harder, man."

Ivor shook him harder and finally something snapped.

A wave of heat raced through him and tingled his fingertips and toes and the moment it did, all sensation returned. He shook his hands and stamped his feet then was off. Down the tunnel, he raced and through the thin crack at the entrance.

Ivor stormed in beside him. "My lady must have compelled me as well. I sensed a daze for a bit, as if I'd caught a wink of sleep or such. Where is she?"

"There is only one place she would go." He glared up at the craggy cliff face, at the hand and footholds and the distinct mark of booted prints grazing the mud coating the black rock. Higher up, the scrub had been tugged on and nearer the ledge that ran in a diagonal line from the halfway point to the top, more signs of her passage lay in the scuffing of her prints, while at his feet, stones and other debris lay scattered in the sand. "She's gone to Dunscaith."

He'd stake his life on it.

"Is all well?" Hamish jogged up from the water's edge where his second had partially beached their vessel along the shoreline. "I caught a vision of Ella falling overboard, but only a mere second afore she did. There was naught I could do to halt her from being tossed into the sea."

"I understand, but now we have an even greater issue. Ella has escaped and climbed by way of this cliff. Sail alongside the coastline as Ivor and I follow her tracks. Watch out for any sign of her."

"Will do." Hamish faced his men. "You heard our orders."

"When I find my wife"—Duncan grasped the first handhold and swung up—"I might very well kill her."

* * * *

Duncan might very well kill her. That thought ricocheted over and over within Ella's mind over the hours following her escape from the cavern. Scaling the cliff hadn't been easy, not with how slick the misty rain had made it, but as her only option she'd taken it after she'd successfully compelled Ivor to ignore her passing.

Determination now spurred her on and she dashed across the craggy hills leading inland and away from the coastline. Duncan would certainly follow her tracks should she leave any, so she'd taken precious minutes to double back where necessary and confuse any markings she'd made. Now, with the cloak of night finally falling, she fled higher into the mountains and raced across the rockier terrain, this land thankfully very familiar to her. She'd trekked it often with both her grandparents, as well as Ethan and Mama.

Water flowed through trickling streams bordered by glistening boulders. Taking extra care with each step, she traversed the stony mountain trail, the odd loose stone shearing away and clacking down into the corrie below, one that lay littered with sand and stones from others who'd passed along this route.

High above, the moon dipped behind wispy cloud floating across it, allowing only the merest trace of moonlight to shimmer through, just enough for her to follow the path. Marching on in her damp clothes, the cold of the night fully descended and surrounded her, the air so very chilly.

Her chest tightened with each step she took farther away from her mate, until her breath became almost too difficult to draw in. Mated pairs always suffered greatly when separated from each other and she'd forced this separation on them both. Not that she'd had a lot of choice. Never would she allow Duncan to lock her away behind Ardan's fortified walls. This was her mission, her kin, and her task to see to.

Through the narrow gorge between the hills, she cut then

stopped to kneel at the edge of a river and gulped down water. The cold hit her belly hard and she shivered anew. Shaking off the bone-deep chill, she pushed to her feet and tramped through the boggy grasses of the marshland leading to the forest bordering her grandparents' cottage.

As the night passed and the dawn sun finally breached the horizon, renewed strength surged through her and she hopped over trailing tree roots along the leaf-strewn forest trail. She strode past a massive pine tree, the trunk three times the size of any other then halted and backed up two steps. Slowly, she circled the familiar trunk.

A mark slashed one side. *E & E*. Memories stirred and a smile lifted her lips. At the age of five and ten, she'd carved hers and Ethan's initials into this tree, gotten told off good and proper by Grandpa too for having done so, but Ethan had adored the inscription she'd made, his toothy ten-year-old grin making the telling-off all the more worth it.

She traced the letters with one finger and hot tears pricked beyond her eyes. She missed Ethan terribly, as well as the man she'd left behind. Nay, she had no time for crying right now. Getting to Dunscaith and aiding Ethan in halting Gavin's attacks was imperative. Her brother was honorable, his desire to ensure peace reigned as strong as hers. No more blood could be shed.

Onward, she trekked until she reached a white arrow painted on the surface of a rock where it sat at the fork in the forest pathway. It pointed to the nearest village, not that she would have missed it. Once she'd walked a trail, she never forgot where it led.

Instead of following the arrow, she took the secondary trail and minutes later emerged from the trees at the edge of a meadow dotted with yellow flowers and lavender bushes. The rising sun washed its golden rays over the thatched rooftop of her grandparents' cottage and such relief filled her. She'd made it this far, and she'd get the rest of the way with her grandparents' aid. They'd never turn her away.

"Grandma, Grandpa!" She raced across the meadow then stopped as two dogs with floppy ears barked from outside the woodshed and tore toward her. The big brutes skidded in beside her, their tongues lolling and eagerness for a pat shining bright in their eyes. She lowered down to her knees and wrapped her arms around their furry necks. "I'm so happy to see you two."

"Ella?" From under the hemp rope strung with clothes between two elm trees, Grandma stood with a cane basket propped against her hip. "Oh my, 'tis you, my dear."

"Aye, 'tis me, Grandma." There was no halting her tears now. They streamed free as she ran and catapulted into Grandma's open arms, the dogs whining at her feet. "I've missed you so much."

"'Tis only been a few weeks, but aye, I've missed you too." Grandma smoothed one hand down the long length of her bedraggled braid. "Look at you, all cold and damp. Clearly you've tramped through the hills to reach us rather than sailed into the harbor at Kinloch. Ewen," she shouted over her shoulder toward the front door of the cottage. "Come see who's here."

"Och, I'm coming." Grandpa sauntered out of the house in his trews and a brown tunic, his hair and beard as thick as always and making him appear ten years younger than the sixty years he held. He grinned, his face lighting up as he caught sight of her. "Our Ella Marie is here."

"I am, but no' without mishap. I have so much to tell you both." She grasped Grandpa and hugged him. "This is one tale you need to hear."

"Come inside then and you can change out of those damp clothes and tell us all about it." He pushed the front door open wider.

"Aye, we'll have you warmed up in no time." Grandma rested a hand at her back and steered her inside and across the main room toward hers and Grandpa's bedchamber. Inside the room with its large bed and burgundy and blue patchwork quilt, Grandma swept the ambry curtain aside and foraged within. "Your voice does no' sound quite right. Why is that?"

"I've no' long recovered from a chill."

"Danger abounds when a compeller loses their voice." Worry flared across Grandma's face as she pulled out a forest-green gown from the back, one which she'd sewn and gifted to Ella on her last birthday. Grandma laid the gown on the bed then hunted some more and pulled out a basket. From the top, she selected a shift and flapped it out. "Disrobe, my dear."

"I'll be glad to do so, even if for a gown." She shucked her coat, shirt, and breeches which had chaffed the insides of her legs, pulled the shift on and sighed as the warmth of the warm cotton encased her.

Next came the gown. With her arms raised, Grandma slid the soft velvet over her head and it shimmered over her hips and swished to her ankles, the low neckline stitched with golden embroidery, the same detailing sewn along the sleeves which draped over the backs of her hands. She slipped her feet into the matching slippers Grandma set at her feet then fastened a golden girdle at her waist, the tasseled ends sweeping down to her knees.

"I'll get these dirtied clothes of yours washed and on the line." Grandma scooped up the pile of clothing and disappeared out the door with it.

She crossed to the window and pressed her hands to the windowsill. The morning sunshine streamed in and flickered over her. At least the storm had now fully passed. She embraced the warmth of this new day, her relief at being here with her most beloved kin, flowing through her. All she'd ever learnt of her skill had been at Grandma's hand. Aye, the two of them held the same skill and during her youth, Grandma had taught her all she'd ever needed to learn in order to wield her ability wisely.

"Come, my dear." Grandma peered around the corner in her

blue woolen kirtle, one hand on the doorway. "A meal awaits us all."

"Coming." She joined her grandparents in the main room and sat at the table near the blazing fire while Grandpa poured warm apple cider into a goblet and passed it to her.

"I'll comb your hair. You've gotten it into an awful mess." Grandma scooped the comb from the kitchen bench and standing at her back, gently worked her knotted plait loose. "Tell me how you've ended up this way. I'm sure 'twill be an interesting tale."

"I'm running from my handfast husband." She sipped the sweet cider.

"Pardon?" Grandma jerked on her hair. "Oh, so sorry, my dear. You surprised me is all. Are you saying you've found your soul bound mate?"

"She better have if she's now wed." Grandpa leaned over the table, cut a slice from the loaf of bread and slathered it in Grandma's delicious raspberry jam before setting it on a plate before her. "We Mathesons certainly dinnae wed those who arenae meant to be ours, that is unless we're certain we are without our chosen one."

"I can only say he's my husband since I've given him my word to keep all his secrets safe. He has quite a few I'm afraid." She didn't doubt that like Ethan, her grandparents too would soon guess that any man she wed must surely hold fae blood. Never would she have wed another over waiting for her chosen one.

"Then we'll presume him to be of fae blood even though you cannae say so." Grandpa dropped into his corner rocking chair, one he'd made himself from a tree he'd felled last winter. Never had she seen another chair like it, the base made of two thick, half-moon shaped wedges attached to the legs. Back and forth, he rocked, his immensely curious gaze locked on her. "Tell us all about your husband and why he isnae here with you right now."

"His name is Duncan MacKenzie and he's the second-born son of the Chief of MacKenzie."

"You have a MacKenzie for a mate?" Grandpa coughed. "You're certain?"

"I'm certain."

"Oh, how interesting." Beaming, Grandma divided her hair into sections then brushed with long, gentle strokes, one foot tapping merrily away at the floor. "Even though our Matheson clan have been at war with the MacKenzies for a very long time, there have still been the odd marriages that have taken place between us over the centuries, that is whenever peace prevailed. How has your Duncan come to hold fae blood, my dear? Through his father or mother?"

"I cannae say." She gave them both a pointed look. "Which will likely be the answer to every question you're going to ask me regarding him."

"Then what can you share?"

"He's loyal, protective, and has already stolen my heart, although last eve I was forced to run away from him."

"Start at the beginning, and tell us all that you can." Grandma notched one brow up, her compelling tone rising to the same sweetly hypnotic tone her own usually did. "I insist, and you know how I like to get my own way."

"Aye, just as I do." With Grandma's compelling command ringing strongly in her ears, Ella began. "Well, so you might understand the turn of events properly. These past few weeks Gavin MacDonald has been causing mayhem, even snuck onto Duncan's land and slaughtered his cattle, as well as set fire to a couple of longhouses at Inverarish, the village under Duncan's care. Ethan is currently with Gavin, has been attempting to halt his devious strikes only he's had no luck. Meanwhile, I've been trying to catch up to them both. I even managed to do so a few days ago, as well as to successfully compel Gavin and demand he return to Dunscaith. Now, I'm to meet Gavin and Ethan there and when I do, I intend on compelling Gavin further as well as speaking to the Chief of MacDonald so I might ensure all is made right. This warring between the clans must stop."

"Gavin has been on a destructive path these past few months." Grandpa leaned forward in his rocking chair, elbows braced to his knees. "This last spring, he even stormed though Kinloch and demanded additional rents be paid, said he did so at his chief's bidding although 'twas naught but a lie." He waved a hand in a rolling motion. "Continue on. What's caused you to leave your husband behind?"

"Duncan fears for my safety, wishes only to send me back to Ardan House and have me locked away, yet 'tis I who must make certain Gavin's attacks are halted, no' him. The last thing I wish to do, is to bring even further harm down upon Duncan's head."

"Och, I see your predicament." Frowning, Grandpa rose and paced the room, his booted feet scuffing the fresh rushes Grandma always scattered about the floors.

"I take it you compelled Duncan in order to sneak away from him?" Grandma patted her shoulder from behind.

"Aye, he left me with no choice."

"There are choices aplenty now." Grandpa braced his hands on his hips as he halted in front of her. "Your grandma and I will travel with you to Dunscaith and aid you in altering Gavin's course, as well as speak to the MacDonald. There is no need for you to tackle this mission alone, no' when you now have us. 'Twill be far easier to see things made right with two compellers at hand."

"'Twill also take us no time at all to sail to Dunscaith." Grandma set her brush down. "We'll leave after you've had some time to rest, Ella. You're clearly exhausted and have been walking right through the night."

"I fear taking the waterways and encountering Duncan. My compelling command willnae halt him forever. 'Twould be best if we rode to Dunscaith."

"Then we'll ride, although we'll need horses if we're to do so." Grandma eyed Grandpa. "We can fetch three mounts from Gregor's stables while Ella rests."

"Agreed. That willnae take us long."

"Then 'tis all sorted." Grandma grasped Ella's hands and tugged her from her chair. Hands on her shoulders, she nudged her down the short hallway toward the spare chamber next to theirs, the room one she'd always used when staying with them.

At the chamber doorway, she blew her grandparents a kiss. Aye, together, they'd sort this out. She had no doubt that they would.

* * * *

High in the craggy hills leading inland, Duncan crouched along a stony trail with Ivor beside him. The ground was soft underfoot, even more so after the squall of yesterday. He touched Ella's booted footprints he'd been following since dawn. Here, the odd clump of loose dirt and gravel had skittered from the pathway down the cliff side and into the corrie below, one strewn with sand and stones.

Last eve, after he and Ivor had found no trace of her passing along the coastline, they'd returned to the cliff where his men had made camp following Hamish's unsuccessful search as well. After a short rest, he'd set out with Ivor to search farther inland. Just the two of them since the last thing he needed was to have all forty of his men tramping across enemy soil and alerting the MacDonald of their arrival on his land. All stealth at present was needed.

Teeth gritted, he studied Ella's tracks deeper. She'd done well to disguise her passage where possible, doubling back in certain places and taking advantage of the streams to conceal her footprints wherever possible. Yet she couldn't hide her final destination. Dunscaith Castle. Even when he'd lost her prints here and there, he'd soon found them again. "We need to catch up to her now."

"Aye, she moves with a faster pace, her footprint slightly deeper." Ivor fingered the mark then pushed to his feet.

Hell, when he found his wayward wife, he'd bind and gag her, bundle her up in his galley and take her directly back to Ardan House where he could lock her away in his bedchamber and ensure she never escaped him again. This mission of hers was perilous, even more so now since she'd set out on her own. One misstep could certainly see her toppling over the side of a ridge and plummeting to her death and that thought, he could barely endure.

Surveying the treacherous path ahead, he trekked on.

As the hours passed, he left the mountainous plateau behind and cut through a narrow gorge in the hills. There, he found the spot where she'd stopped to kneel at the edge of a river for a drink, her knee prints firm in the sandy soil. Although, she hadn't crossed the fast-flowing waters here, her prints moving on alongside the bank. He scooped water and drank, his satchel strapped to his back, Ella's too since he'd grabbed it before leaving the temporary camp he and his men had set up at the bay.

Back on the sodden trail, he picked up his pace, Ivor one step behind him.

Striding through the boggy grasses, he remained alert as he scanned their surroundings. Soon, he left the marshland behind and jogged through the forest and along a leaf strewn trail. He trotted past a massive pine tree with a trunk at least three times the size of any other and stopped.

Something about it intrigued him and he turned back. Roaming around it, he spied engraved letters scored into the bark and gently, he traced the etched markings. *E & E.*

On the ground, Ella's booted marks showed she'd stopped here as well.

"Ella and Ethan," he bit out to Ivor. The initials could easily stand for such. "We're close, very close."

Picking up his pace, he ran until he reached a divide in the path. A white arrow painted on the surface of a rock pointed straight ahead, likely to Kinloch harbor, although 'twas the path veering to the right that held her firm print. Her grandparents lived close to the harbor. She'd said they resided only a day's ride from Dunscaith. That would make this spot as being about right.

He took the trail she had, the midday sunshine streaming through the canopy overhead and flecking golden rays over the path holding thick scrub either side and snaking tree roots. Birds twittered from high in their nests, their chirps echoing through the woods in a high-pitched chorus.

Onward, he stormed then halted as the forest suddenly gave way to a small clearing dotted with yellow flowers and thick clumps of grass. Smoke curled into the air from a cottage with a thatched rooftop while clothes fluttered on a rope hung between two elm trees.

Amongst those clothes a very familiar pair of navy breeches and a brown rawhide coat dried. Ella's clothes. Relief swamped him, right along with a fierce bolt of need to find her and gather her close in his arms.

Sword unsheathed, he snuck across the meadow toward the front door and tested the handle. It turned with ease and the door creaked open. All remained eerily quiet inside. A fire blazed along one wall near a table with two chairs and a bench tucked underneath it. Ella's riding boots sat propped in front of the hearth and as he crouched near the table, he picked up a strand of her brown hair. Aye, very close indeed.

In the kitchen tucked to one side of the main room, pots and utensils hung from hooks and a larder sat recessed into a darkened nook. He crept, across freshly scented rushes and past an open door leading to a bedchamber with a soft burgundy and blue patchwork quilt. No one remained within the room, the sunshine streaming through the window and dappling across the covers.

He continued on toward the chamber door at the far end of the passageway. It remained closed, but all his instincts blared that he'd find his chosen one within that room.

Over his shoulder, he gestured for Ivor to await him outside and to maintain a tight guard. No one would keep his wife from him a moment longer, not even Ella herself.

Chapter 9

The lightest creak of the floorboards outside her bedchamber door stirred Ella from her sleep. She stretched and opened her eyes. Grandma and Grandpa must have returned. Covers tossed back, she eased out of bed and straightened her forest-green skirts then popped her slippers on.

She made the door just as it swung open and Duncan filled the frame.

Goodness. Her jaw dropped and her mouth dried out. The renewed sight of him took her breath away, his tan leather vest studded with bits of steel stretching tight across his broad shoulders, his leather-covered legs braced wide apart. "W-what are you doing here?" He should never have been able to catch up to her this fast.

"You. Left. Me." He closed the door behind him, heaved her up against the wall and pressed his big body against every inch of hers. "I take it this your grandparents' cottage?"

"Aye, and they'll be back soon, right after they've run an errand. They're collecting mounts from the harbor village for our ride to Dunscaith. I willnae be alone in my coming mission. Grandma is a compeller and they've both agreed two compellers will be stronger than one. I'll ensure Gavin is halted, as will my grandparents as well."

"You're no' going anywhere near Dunscaith. My decision at the cavern still stands." He hauled his belt free, grasped her hands together and strapped the thick leather around her wrists before cinching it tight. "You'll be locked away within Ardan's walls where no harm can possibly come to you. Ivor is with me and he too will ensure that is so."

"Duncan, you cannae bind me in this way."

"I am, and I have." From his pocket, he pulled out a wad of cloth and stuffed it in her mouth then wrapped a length of tartan around her head to keep it in place. "'Twill be I alone who deals with Gavin MacDonald. Am I understood?"

"Nay," she mumbled into the cloth and pushed the wad free with her tongue, his binding around her mouth not nearly as tight as he should have made it to keep it in place. "Dinnae do to me as your father did to your mother. He kept her bound and contained. I willnae allow you to keep me as your prisoner, nor beat down my spirit and control me." Squirming for release, she lashed out and swung her leg.

He blocked her kick with his leg, stuffed the wad of cloth back into her mouth then moved to tighten the knot at the back of her head, but suddenly stilled, his hands shaking and agony flaring across his face. "You truly believe I'm treating you just as my father so badly treated my mother?"

She spat the wad back out and the strip slipped down to her neck. "You are treating me as if you own me, wishing only to bend me to your will. Duncan, you dinnae have your father's devious nature, only your mother's strong heart. What did Beth want when she learnt of your father's true intent?"

"To run from him."

"Do you wish for me to desire the same as well? To run from you."

"Nay, never." Stumbling back a step, such anguish pooled in his eyes. "What am I doing?"

"You only wish to keep me safe and I understand your need, but I am no' a lass you can easily bend to your will. Remove my bindings." She gentled her tone, searched his gaze and stuck her hands out toward him. "No man who truly loves his wife would ever bind her in such a way."

"You're right." Disgust laced his tone and he hauled the binding from her hands free, his hands still shaking as he shoved back and paced the room. "I'm so sorry, Ella. You deserve a far better husband than me."

"You are the only man I want"—she stepped in his path, halted him in place—"but most of all, I want your trust. I can see to this mission and bring Gavin's destructive strikes to a stop. You must believe in me, have faith that I can do as I've said."

"I understand your skill is strong, but even so I still fear for your safety. You can never halt that from arising. You also ran away from me, and that I can never allow again."

"I agree running was no' wise, but you truly left me with no other choice. If you promise me that you'll never bind me in such a way again, I promise to never run." Needing him so desperately, likely as he needed her too, she worked the ties on his pants loose and freed his cock, which hardened and pushed eagerly into her hands. "Do we have an agreement?"

"Aye, we do." He hoisted up her skirts and thrust into her, so fast she almost lost her breath. "By the way, you forgive far too quickly."

"Oh my." Filled to the brim with him, she clutched his broad shoulders, this moment so sweetly necessary. "'Tis worth forgiving quickly to ensure this kind of joining."

"I couldnae stand our parting." He gripped her backside, lifted her up and dropped her back down on top of him.

"Mmm, neither could I. Do that again."

"I am so fortunate to have you as mine." Growling low in his throat, he took possession of her mouth, his kiss thrilling as he thrust his tongue between her lips and did exactly as she'd asked. He thrust into her, over and over until she moaned her pleasure.

* * * *

Duncan tried to pull himself back, to not take Ella so madly against the wall, only her forgiveness made his need for her roar though with such fierce intensity. As he pounded into her, he tugged the low neckline of her gown down and lifted one breast free. Head dipped, he suctioned his mouth around the hard nipple, his desire to mark and brand her with his kisses all that drove him. He tasted and devoured her and she thrashed against him, her gasps for more sending him half crazed. With his pants sliding to his knees and her bottom in his hands, he tumbled her to the floor.

"You're heavy, Duncan." She squirmed underneath him. "Let me up on top."

"Sorry, love." He rolled her with him as he moved onto his back and she sat up over top of him, straddled his hips and rocked him ever deeper inside her. "Aye, that's it. Ride me and dinnae stop," he demanded.

"I intend to." She gasped as she moved up and down over him, taking his shaft deep into the heavenly heart of her core. "Oh, aye, this I love."

"I'm going to lose my mind."

"Then let's hope you lose the part that cannae deal with my need for freedom." She arched her back as she picked up her speed.

The intensity of the moment shook him and he grasped her hips, rocked them even harder together until her tight channel swamped him in such sweet pressure as she hugged him all the way to his balls.

"Duncan, I cannae hold on any longer."

"Neither can I. Let go. I'm right here with you, always with you."

"In this need we are the same." She cried out her pleasure,

her inner channel pulsing around his cock and with no choice left to him, he came hard and fast, his seed shooting to her core as he shattered right along with her.

Hell, he couldn't move, his limbs so heavy and his body saturated with pleasure. 'Twas as if she'd drained his life's blood and not on the battlefield but on the hard floorboards of her grandparents' cottage. Such control she wielded over him and always would.

With her slumped on top of him, he ran one hand down her back and over her long, loose locks. The silky brown strands slid between his fingers. "Ella," he murmured in her ear, "I have no desire to beat down your spirit and control you."

"I'm aware." She lifted up a touch, both her breasts now swaying free and her forest-green skirts bunched between them. "Let us return to the plan we made at the inn. We'll both head to Dunscaith, Ivor as well since you said he came with you. You'll both don hooded cloaks and Grandma and I will compel any unwanted attention away from you both. We'll remain at Dunscaith for no longer than is absolutely necessary."

"I can agree to that. We'll be in and out, as quick as we can." He cupped the back of her head and brought her mouth back to within an inch of his. "Kiss me again, and dinnae stop."

"If I kiss you"—she pressed her fingers to his mouth— "we'll never get off this floor."

"The bed is fairly close and I'm certain I can make it there."

She giggled and shook her head. "My grandparents are due back at any moment. I told them all about you, although no' of your fae blood. Unfortunately though, they've guessed all the same. They know I'd never wed a man unless a bond had formed between us."

"They're aware we've spoken handfast vows, that you chose to run from me?"

"Aye." She rolled off him, flipped her skirts back down as she lay on her back and stared at the planked ceiling, an inquisitive look on her face.

"What are you thinking?" He eased onto his side, slid the sleeves of forest-green gown farther down her arms and palmed her breasts. Head bent, he licked each pebbled tip and reveled in the taste of her. Like a fine wine, he wanted to get drunk on her and gently, he suckled one aureole deep inside his mouth then moved to the other and flicked the tip with his tongue.

"Duncan?" Lashes fluttering down, she moaned.

"Tell me what you're thinking."

"About naught but you at the moment. You always scramble my thoughts."

"My laird?" A knock and Ivor's voice echoed through the door. "My lady's grandparents have returned from Kinloch harbor with three mounts and wish to ensure their granddaughter is well. They also dinnae seem very surprised to find us here."

"We'll be out in a moment."

"Tell them I'm well, Ivor. Very well." Ella lifted her sleeves embellished with golden embroidery back up her arms, slipped her breasts inside the bodice and as she sat up, adjusted her golden girdle at her waist.

He pushed to his feet, straightened his own clothing and offered her a hand. "I seem to be falling into your plans with far more ease than I thought possible during my trek here. Can I ask if you've compelled me since my arrival?"

"I've compelled naught of you." Laughing, she reached up on her toes and wrapped her arms around his neck. "You've simply seen reason, which is what happens to a man when he discovers his mate talks sense."

"When do you wish to leave for Dunscaith?" He detested losing this precious time with her, but with this fine weather, Gavin would be on the move and they needed to reach the MacDonald's stronghold as soon as possible.

"Once you've had a short rest." She traced her thumbs under his eyes. "I dinnae care for these black circles and you need to be at your most alert while journeying across MacDonald land. We'll depart closer to dusk. Traveling the roads during the dark will also ensure less notice is drawn to you and Ivor. There will be no harm in waiting a few more hours. Do you agree?"

"Aye, agreed." He rubbed against her, surrounded himself in her delicious womanly scent. Sweet vanilla swirled around him and his cock twitched and rose back to life. "I want to be buried deep inside you again."

"I want that too, but for now, come and meet my kin." She towed him to the door and swished out into the main room.

Next to the fireplace, an elderly man with thick hair and a beard sat in an unusual chair, the base made of two half-moon shaped wooden wedges attached to the legs. Chair creaking, he rocked back and forth, his hands curled around the smooth wooden armrests and his gaze moving from Ella to him and back to Ella again. In dark trews and a brown tunic, the man nodded as if what he saw pleased him. "You're Duncan, I take it?"

"Aye, and I apologize for my unannounced arrival."

"Think naught of it." He waved his concern away. "My granddaughter appears content now, no' as anxious as she did this morn upon her arrival. Your man, Ivor, explained your trek here to us. Welcome to our home, Duncan. I'm Ewen." He gestured to Ella's grandma sitting at the table, her gray hair piled high upon her head and her blue woolen skirts fluffed around her. "This is my wife, Marie."

"'Tis good to meet you both."

"'Tis lovely to meet you too, Duncan." Marie offered him a wide smile.

"Duncan and I have spoken." Ella crossed to her grandpa, popped a kiss on his cheek then popped another on her grandma's cheek as well. "Both he and Ivor will be traveling with us to Dunscaith, both with a hooded cloak to disguise themselves. Grandma, you and I will need to compel any unwanted attention away from them both should they garner any."

"Aye, that I can easily do." Marie nodded.

Ewen rocked back and forth in his chair. "We'll need to secure another two mounts for the ride. 'Twill be easily enough done though."

"We've decided to leave at dusk and travel the roads during the dark of night. Less notice will be drawn to us if we do." Ella glanced at Duncan. "Are you hungry, my stubborn one?"

"Famished." He winked at her and she blushed.

"Naughty husband. I didnae mean that kind of hunger." She caught his hand, led him to the bench seat before the table and continued on to the kitchen. "Sit and talk to Grandma while I rustle us all up a meal."

"Aye, I would like to speak to them about my birth and how I came to be your husband." Ivor remained outside so he could do so without the knowledge going any further than the four of them. Ella trusted her grandparents and so too would he. No more secrets. Not with her most beloved kin.

Eyes alight, Ella picked up the jug and poured cider into four tankards and set the drinks on the table. She rummaged about in the cupboards and laid out platters of food. Bread, cheeses and a selection of meats, a pot of raspberry jam and a tub of honey too.

She was so at home here, just as he wished for her to be at home at Ardan House, the lady of his keep as she oversaw all. Her grandparents too followed her every move, love shining bright in their eyes. How he wanted to meet her mama and brother as well, to ensure all her nearest and dearest were aware they'd always be welcome at his home, no matter he was a MacKenzie and currently their clan's greatest enemy.

The door squeaked open and Ivor eyed him from the doorway. "Is all well?"

"Aye. We'll leave at dusk. Rest as you can, but keep a close eye on all outside as well."

"Wait a moment, Ivor." Ella laid slivers of beef on a thick slice of bread, added cheese and a handful of nuts to the side of the plate then handed it to his man along with a drink. "If you need more, return and help yourself. My grandma thrives on keeping her larder full of food, always has plenty for those who might visit."

"Thank you, my lady." With a quick bow to her and then to Marie, he slipped outside with his food and shut the door behind himself.

Ella squeezed Duncan's shoulder as she sat, then nudged his tankard closer. "Drink."

A compelled command and he sipped his mulled cider, the delectable brew sliding down his parched throat. He licked his lips, the drink both apple-sweet and cinnamon-spicy, but there was something else."

"'Tis delicious, dinnae you think?" Under the table, Ella stroked his leg, her fingers sliding around his inner thigh and moving perilously close to his cock which once again ached for more of her touch. "Grandma adds a secret ingredient to the apple cider, one I'm afraid she'll never spill the details about, although Mama knows exactly how to make it too. Unfortunately, I've never learnt."

"Then your kin will need to visit us at Ardan House and ensure the barrels are filled with this brew."

"They'd like that." Smiling, she looked deeper into his eyes.

"We certainly would." Ewen rose from his rocking chair and settled on the bench seat next to Marie. He slathered a crusty slice of bread with honey and folded it in two, his curious gaze on him. "Tell us all about yourself, yet only speak the secrets you truly wish to."

"My twin brother and I both hold fae blood." The words passed his lips easily.

"You can trust us, son, just as you trust your mate. No' a

word you speak of this day shall leave our lips." A firm nod from Ewen.

Son? The term rang with endearment, one his father had never even issued with him.

"My mother's name was Beth and many years ago she journeyed from the fae village to my father's keep." He'd share it all. "At the time Colin MacKenzie desired fae blood flowing within his direct line, but with his betrothal agreement already signed with the daughter of his neighboring clan's chief, his hope to fulfil that desire remained beyond his reach. Or at least until he caught sight of Beth and chose a rather devious path. He spoke handfast vows with her then once she'd conceived, he had her locked within his chamber and none permitted entry other than one single maid."

Ella leaned into his side, rubbed her cheek against his arm.

He slid his dirk free, cut two slices from the loaf and laid them on their plate. After adding meat and cheese to each slice, he lifted one to Ella's lips and ensured she took a bite. Looking into her eyes, he murmured, "I wish my mother had never perished in order to give Coll and I life, wish she'd been there to raise us, to teach us all about our Matheson kin, but that was never to be."

"She might no' have been given that chance, but her spirit still lives on in you and Coll, and now we're wed, I will surely be here to teach you all you wish to know about your Matheson kin. My grandparents will too. Mama and Ethan as well. You need never be alone again."

"I dinnae know what I did to deserve you." Cupping her cheek, he pressed a kiss to her lips.

"You're my husband, my mate." She smiled, the gold flecks rimming her brown eyes lighting with such stunning brilliance. "The only one who'll ever hold the other half of my soul."

"I wish to wed you proper."

"I wouldnae mind that either." Her grin widened.

"Here, here," Ewen cheered and Marie clapped. "Duncan, you and your brother are our kin. Never forget that."

"Thank you." Their welcome was one he embraced with all his heart.

Chapter 10

"You're supposed to be resting so we can leave once you have." At the edge of the meadow where the late afternoon sunshine beamed through the leaves and sprinkled over the ground, Ella unpegged the clothes from the line.

"I thought we agreed I would, provided you laid down with me." Duncan's billowy white tunic, untucked under his tan leather vest studded with steel, lifted in the brisk breeze and gave a delicious glimpse of the twin lines of roped muscle rippling either side of his abs. She wanted to run her hands over his exposed flesh then loosen the ties of his tan rawhide pants which clung to his trim hips and shimmy them down his legs.

Instead, she sighed and continued unpegging the clothes. "You'll never get any rest if I join you in bed. Once I've brought Grandma's washing in, I'll take a nap in their chamber since I could still use a little more sleep."

"I'm a man starved for his wife. Have mercy on me." He caught her around the waist, lifted her off her feet and held her flush against him, her toes dangling an inch from the ground.

"Put me down, Duncan." Giggling, she swatted his arm. "And I believe I quenched your thirst upon your arrival."

"You didnae quench it nearly enough for my liking." He

twirled her around behind the closest tree then pressed her against the wide trunk and thankfully out of sight of Ivor patrolling the far side of the meadow. Leaning in, he caged her in place, his palms lying flat against the rough bark either side of her head. "I'm in love with my wife, want her with a desperate desire that willnae be abated."

"I'm in love with you too, but I need you to be at your clearest of mind as we travel to Dunscaith. Only adequate rest will ensure that." She jabbed a finger into his chest, tried to give him her sternest look but only failed terribly. "Sheer exhaustion isnae permitted."

"Sheer exhaustion sounds divine, particularly if offered at your hands." Sweetly sensual words whispered in her ear, his breath fluttering strands of her loose hair.

"Goodness, what am I going to do with you?" She snuck her fingers under the flapping hem of his tunic and stroked over his sides.

"Keep touching me and we'll see." He stroked one finger along the low neckline of her gown.

"All I want to do is keep you close." She played with one of his pant ties while overhead, a bird squawked then landed in the canopy and hopped into its nest. All around her the scents of the forest swirled, bringing with it the fresh aroma of pine mixed with the dampness of the earth, although Duncan's deliciously warm and spicy scent stamped itself over it all.

"I will always long for you, Ella." His deep voice rumbled with hunger, his blue eyes darkening with lust.

She melted against him, her legs all wobbly. All she wanted to do was rip his clothes from him and topple him to the forest floor. "You've stolen my heart, Duncan MacKenzie, and I never wish for you to hand it back."

"You have mine as well." Breathing raggedly, he brushed her cheeks with the backs of his hands. "Do you want me right now, the same way I want you?"

"Aye, but we arenae alone out here. Ivor is close." She rubbed against the heat of his formidably muscled body. Never could she ever deny him what he truly wished for, and right now that appeared to be her.

"There is naught more precious than this mated bond and the depth it grows between us." He bent his head, trailed kisses along her jaw then when he reached her ear, sucked her lobe into his mouth.

"Well, well, who do we have here?" In a black war coat glinting with studded steel, Gavin MacDonald stepped out from behind a tree. Heavily armed and fully prepared for battle, his claymore sat snugly in his fisted hand while daggers shone from both his wrists. "You spoke of a bond, MacKenzie, the mated bond of the fae I take it? Only how is it such a bond could have formed between the two of you? She's a Matheson and you're a MacKenzie."

"How one formed is of no concern of yours." Growling under his breath, Duncan left her behind and advanced on Gavin.

"Yet I am intrigued all the same." Gavin charged forward and Duncan slid his sword free and thrust high. Their two blades crashed together, steel slamming hard into steel and the resounding clang echoed all around. "Did you come by way of it through your mother's line or your father's line, I wonder?"

"Again, 'tis of no concern of yours."

Across the meadow the roar of two warriors meeting head on boomed toward Ella and she ducked around the tree and clutched her chest. Ivor swung his sword at another MacDonald and the chickens roaming freely near the henhouse squawked and flapped out of the way.

Nay. She had to halt this fight right—

"You're coming with me." A hand clamped around her mouth and one of Gavin's men hauled her farther away from Duncan and shoved her up against a trunk. Her head hit hard and black dots hazed her vision. She fought to clear her muddled thoughts. She had to get Duncan's attention, and she definitely needed to free herself, use her voice to halt this coming battle. Never would she allow blood to be shed here this day.

"My men and I will dispatch both you and your guardsman." Gavin spat at Duncan's feet then slashed again, the two men barely visible through the trees. "Then I'll gather an even larger fighting force and sail for Ardan House. I shall take your holding for myself since you willnae be there to halt me."

"You go too far." Duncan twirled as another of Gavin's warriors bounded out and came in on the other side of him. The three fought, Duncan meeting first Gavin's blow then swinging at the other warrior.

Her captor dragged her ever deeper into the woods and away. She thrashed and tried to scream, but her shout was naught more than a feeble mumble against his meaty palm.

A fierce roar reverberated and she just caught a glimpse of Ivor jumping over low scrub and skidding in beside Duncan before she was hauled behind several thick bushes. At least her mate now had aid.

"Ella!" Duncan's bellow cut through the forest and sent birds cackling and soaring high into the sky.

She tried to call out, to fight the thug who'd taken her, but he pinned her to the ground and dropped down on top of her. His fetid breath washed over her, his hand still firm on her mouth as he flipped her skirts. He freed his cock from his pants, grasped his stiff shaft and she writhed, tried desperately to kick him where it ought to hurt.

"Get off my wife." A blood-curdling battle cry ricocheted all around and Duncan slammed his blade into the warrior. Blood sprayed and the man toppled off her.

"Ella, did he hurt you?" Duncan swept her to her feet and into his arms, the man unmoving on the ground.

"I'm fine. You arrived in time." She dragged in a deep breath. "Go and aid Ivor."

"No' without you." He tossed her over one shoulder and ran back with her toward the raging battle.

"Watch out." Ethan bounded down the trail and head down, plowed into another of Gavin's men flying toward them with his blade raised high. Ethan and the man crashed to the ground and blood spurted, Ethan's dagger embedded deep within the warrior's gut.

"Ethan." She scrambled out of Duncan's hold and grasped Ethan's shoulders, his pants slashed down one leg. "We have to stop Gavin."

"Aye, and right this moment."

"You remain here, Ethan. I'll return to the fight. Look after my wife." Duncan left her with her brother, surged toward the battling men and bounded into the battle.

* * * *

Duncan jumped the low brush and swung at Gavin as he and his warrior fought Ivor. He hadn't wished to leave Ivor in such a predicament, but when he'd turned around and found Ella gone, he'd made chase after whoever had taken her. Never would she have run from a fight and he'd feared the worst, had barely gotten to her in time. The sight of that thug about to surge into her had made his fury soar, his strike a death blow.

Rocking from foot to foot, he caught Gavin's next blow then ducked low, whipped his blade into Gavin's side before striking another of Gavin's warriors who jumped into the fray.

"Pin him between us." Gavin grasped his side, the long cut in his heavily padded jerkin drawing blood as he snarled at his man. "We'll slay MacKenzie where he stands. Three, two, one."

Their blades descended.

Hell. Duncan spun, caught both well-timed blows above his head, his arms shaking as he held his position. Swiftly, he kicked Gavin off balance then swept his other leg out and toppled the other man. Both fell forward, their claymores sliding down each other's and impaling the other's chest. Blood gurgled from their mouths and Gavin's eyes went wide before flickering shut as he slumped into a heap, his lifeblood flowing into the dirt.

Beside him, Ivor slammed his blade into the MacDonald warrior he fought, metal clanging, his strike so harsh it sent the man toppling sideways and he fell and hit his head on a protruding rock next to a thorny bush. Skin split open and blood sprayed, the hit far too deadly for it not to have taken his life.

"Oh goodness." Ella clutched a hand to her mouth as Ethan crouched next to Gavin. He rolled him and the other slain warrior over, took one look at both men and shook his head at his sister.

"This is all my fault." Ella dropped to her knees next to Ethan, her face turning white.

Ivor hunkered down beside the warrior he'd fought, held his palm to the man's mouth and with a shake of his head, said, "He willnae rise, and neither shall the other warrior who attacked me across the meadow." Ivor grimaced, grasped his side, blood oozing from a cut. "They intended our death this day. 'Twas either them or us."

"Are you all right?" Duncan aided Ella to her feet with his hands around hers and shielded her with his body as he searched the surrounding tree line. "Ethan, are all the men traveling with Gavin accounted for?"

"Another warrior joined us on the trek here. There's one miss—duck." Ethan jumped to his feet, flung his dirk and sent it spinning end over end right toward him. Duncan dropped to the ground with Ella as the blade whizzed over their heads and *thunked* into another MacDonald warrior slinking out from the tree right behind them. The man's raised blade clattered to the ground, Ethan's dirk now buried deep between his eyes as he crumpled into a heap, death taking him swift and fast. "Aye, now all are accounted for," Ethan muttered.

"What of you?" Ella swept her hands over Duncan. "Are you hurt?"

"I'm fine, love."

With no other MacDonalds in sight, he ran his hands over her body, touched the scrapes on her arms and her ripped sleeve. No other nicks or cuts. She remained clear of any injury, although needing a moment to calm his raging fear for her, he clutched her tight. He should never have let his guard down while on MacDonald land, no matter being within a stone's throw of her grandparents' cottage.

Ethan strode past them and looked over Ivor's wound. "How bad is it?"

"I might need a few stitches, although I've suffered far worse than this afore. Are you certain we can expect no more men to suddenly appear?" Ivor searched through the trees.

"Very certain. I'm sorry I couldnae get here sooner to warn you all." Ethan eyed Duncan. "Gavin caught sight of your galley sailing down the kyle and decided 'twas time for the hunter to become the hunted. I crossed the hills with him as he snuck after you, then when I realized his intent, that there was naught I could do to halt his desire for this battle, I fought him and he had me bound and gagged then tied high in a tree."

"You arrived in time to aid us and for that I'm most grateful." Gently, Duncan rubbed Ella's back as he held her, his very soul demanding further retribution against the warrior who'd tried to hurt her, only the man had already paid with his life.

"We need to see to the burial of all those who've perished here this day." Ethan touched Ella on the back and she slid out of Duncan's hold and hugged her brother. Ethan whispered in her ear, "Tend to Ivor's wound while Duncan and I dig a pit."

"Of course." Shaking, she stepped across to Ivor and the two left.

Duncan watched her as she walked across the meadow and disappeared inside the cottage. Once assured she remained safe within her grandparents' home, he turned to Ethan. "I truly thank you for your timely arrival and aid in the battle."

"I never wished for this fight. Certainly when the MacDonald learns of this battle and his nephew's death, he'll come after you."

"I've no doubt the war between our clans is about to get a hell of a lot bloodier." He gripped Ethan's shoulder. "I'll make things right. Never will I allow you, your sister or your grandparents to suffer any injustice because of what's happened here this day."

The reek of death now pervaded this place, as well as cast a heavy pall of darkness over them all. Aye, Gavin had paid with his life for his misdeeds, but so too would Duncan pay for the danger he'd brought down upon his wife's head.

A danger he could never permit.

Above all else, Ella's safety came first, no matter the cost to him.

Chapter 11

Inside the cottage, Ella tended to Ivor, cleaned and stitched his wound then burst into tears when her grandparents walked in the door and looked so stricken. She rushed across to them and Grandma bundled her up in her arms, a warm haven of strength within the storm of her emotions. She sobbed at the loss of life, babbled her distress at having brought such a battle to their doorstep, right here where she'd experienced only wonderful times. "I'm so sorry."

"Duncan and Ethan met us in the meadow, told us all that had happened." Grandma held her close.

"Gavin and his men's deaths were inevitable from what we've been told." Grandpa kissed the top of Ella's head then nodded at Grandma. "I'll go and aid Duncan and Ethan with the burials."

"I'll come with you." Ivor rose from the seat where she'd tended him, his gaze on Grandpa. "The MacDonald will never allow his men's deaths to pass without seeking retribution against those who had a hand in it."

"Aye, I agree. Duncan also mentioned the same to my wife and I. He's come up with a plan to deal with it." Grandpa grasped Ivor's shoulder. "Come, we'll join the others now."

"Stay right here." Ivor cast her a look and when she nodded, he followed Grandpa out the door.

"Ivor is right. The MacDonald will certainly wish to seek his retribution against us all, and since we cannae change what has happened here this day, then we must prepare for what is to come." Grandma rubbed her back, her words a soft murmur in her ear.

"I fear that retribution."

"As do I. Come and sit." Grandma urged her down into Grandpa's rocking chair then knelt at the hearth, added another block of peat and once it had caught alight, dusted her hands against her kirtle's blue skirts and rose. Frowning, Grandma pulled the three-legged stool from the corner closer and squeezed her knee. "A burden shared is a burden halved. Speak to me."

"So many lives have been lost here this day and all because I chose to come and seek shelter with you." Knees pulled to her chest, she wrapped her arms around them and rocked. Her heart ached, so bad. "All I ever wished to do was prevent such blood from being shed, no' to have been the cause of it. I've dishonored Papa's memory this day."

"You've done no such thing, and I willnae have you think otherwise."

"This is all such a mess."

"The battle that occurred this day, and the deaths that came from it, were both unfortunate and unnecessary, but Duncan and Ivor did naught more than defend themselves, Ethan too in his need to halt the men seeking to attack you and your mate so underhandedly." Grandma clasped her chilled hands, such sadness crossing her face. "While outside, Duncan spoke to your grandpa and I. He believes there is only one line of defense now open to us."

"We cannae tell the MacDonald of Duncan's involvement in this battle. He'll come after him."

"Duncan intends to take full responsibility for all that's

happened, and to ensure the rest of us remain clear of any involvement." Grandma's gaze softened. "You must allow him to do so. There's no other way we can move forward if we all wish to survive the Chief of MacDonald's coming wrath."

"Excuse me." Duncan stood inside the open doorway, water dripping from his hands and face where he'd scrubbed up at the water barrel outside. To her grandma, he said, "May I have a moment to speak to my wife in private? I need to do so afore I leave."

"Of course, and know that we dinnae blame you for what has happened here this day." Tears welling in Grandma's eyes, she hugged Duncan then shuffled outside.

Her chosen one shut the door, the quiet *snick* reverberating like thunder in her ears. From beside the door, he collected his and Ivor's satchels, although he left her bag sitting there as he made his way to her. "By my actions this day, I've endangered your life and that of your loved ones."

"You did naught more than defend yourself. I'm the one at fault. I led you and Gavin right here." Hot tears burned behind her eyes and slowly slid down her cheeks.

"Nay, my love, death pervades this place because of me, and once the MacDonald hears of all that's happened here this day, I'll have gained an even greater enemy than I already have. Right now, above all things, your safety and that of your kin must come first." Pain slashed his face. "It has been decided. Ewen and Ethan will both ride to Dunscaith, speak to the MacDonald and inform him of all that's happened, that I alone am responsible for slaying Gavin and his men. 'Twas simply most unfortunate that it occurred right here on your grandparents' doorstep. That is the only way to clear them of any involvement."

"The MacDonald will come after you."

"Aye, but you'll be safe, just as safe as you've always been, provided you no longer hold my name and that the MacDonald never learns we were wed. Fortunately, all those now aware of our bond lie below the ground, and at least that I can be grateful for."

"You cannae think to leave me." She heaved to her feet, her legs trembling. "I'm coming with you."

"You need to remain here." He strode to the door, halted and glanced over his shoulder at her, his expression tortured. "We are no longer wed. I repudiate my handfast vow." Broken words, and each one tore at her heart.

"You cannae do this to us. After all we've been through, you truly wish to give up on our bond? No more marriage?"

"Ensuring your safety is imperative, and this is the only way to do so. Deep inside your heart, you know it too. There can be no more bond. I'll never allow the MacDonald to use you or your kin as pawns in our war."

"There has to be another way, Duncan." Anger and frustration crashed fiercely inside her, made her heart cry out with the pain of her loss.

"There is none."

"Dinnae leave me." She wanted to scream and hit him, only she remained frozen and still.

"I love you, will always love you."

"And I hate you," she slammed back at him. How could he leave her like this? Just utter a few simple words and end their handfast and toss any possible future away.

"Farewell, Ella." He shut the door and was gone.

She sank to the ground, never more lost and alone, her heart crushed.

* * * *

We are no longer wed. I repudiate my handfast vow.

Duncan's final words continued to reverberate through Ella's mind each day over the torturously long month that followed, the pain of his rejection never easing. Her chest burned where her heart had been, every day one in which she struggled to rise, woodenly saw to her chores which Grandma had set while Ethan moped around too. After the battle, Grandpa and Ethan had ridden to Dunscaith Castle and told the MacDonald what Duncan had instructed them to say, that he alone was responsible for his nephew and men's deaths. The MacDonald chief had been furious, had sent out a band of his men to seek adequate justice and a mighty battle had ensued along the shores of Loch Carron near Ardan House.

Word had reached her in the following days, that even more men had lost their lives, a war that still raged even now.

"I know exactly how you're feeling, my sweet." Mama swished across the meadow toward where she lay in the long grass. Grandpa had sailed for the village and returned with Mama within days of Duncan's leaving. Ever since, Mama had been trying to raise her spirits. Plopping down beside her in her red skirts, such sympathy and love shone in her parent's eyes. "I hate to see you in such pain, Ella."

"Each day seems excruciatingly endless." She fisted the long grass while overhead wispy clouds floated past. "How did you survive without Papa?"

"All I wanted to do was curl up and die, but you and Ethan kept me sane until one day, I suddenly began to remember the good times and no longer focused on the bad. You must no' forget that your mate still lives, that you have no' lost him as I lost your papa. Take comfort in that."

"The last words I threw at him still haunt me."

"What did you say?"

"That I hated him." Despair overwhelmed her, made each breath she took come harder.

"Deep in his heart, he knows the truth." Mama laid a hand on her arm, stroked back and forth. "Your grandma and I have been speaking."

"There is no child, Mama." They'd both given her expectant looks this past week after she'd heaved up her morning meal each day. "You must cease saying so, or thinking so."

"I couldnae eat either when I first conceived you and Ethan. Grandma too was the same when she carried her bairns. You also have no' had your courses since your handfast."

"Aye, but that means naught." She laid a hand over her flat belly.

"Then what does it mean, my obstinate daughter?"

"Mama, I am no' obstinate." Huffing, she sat up in her breeches and tunic then swayed with dizziness at having moved so fast. Taking a deep breath, she steadied herself. "He does no' want me anymore."

"You love him."

"He left me. Repudiated his vow and ended our handfast. If I'm to have his child, the poor thing will never hold his name, be known only as a bastard."

"Aye, but the child will still be loved by us all. Never forget that." Mama waved to Grandma who stood leaning against the doorway. "She still willnae listen to reason."

"I'm listening perfectly fine." She thumped the grass. "There is no child."

"There is, my dear." Grandma smiled as she sat with a flourish of her kirtle's maroon skirts. "'Tis clear to see. We also all agree that we cannae allow Duncan to never hear news of the babe you're carrying, or of its coming birth. 'Twould be wrong, very wrong."

"I'm no' allowed anywhere near Duncan, so that makes telling him impossible."

"Duncan didnae have a choice but to repudiate your vow and leave." Grandma plucked a yellow flower from the grass and tucked it behind Ella's ear. "He had to accept what followed, just as we all did."

"He took my heart and left me with naught but a gaping hole where it should be." Gently, reverently, she pressed a hand to her belly, her breath stuttering in and out. She longed to have a part of Duncan to hold onto, a child with his beautiful blue eyes and her feisty temperament. Aye, she'd love naught more.

"We could sail for Ardan House this night, all of us, but only under the cover of darkness." Grandma cupped her cheek. "We'll ensure we remain disguised so no one can make us out on the water. Then we'll return again once you've imparted your news. There and back in one night. It can be done."

Just to see him one more time would likely kill her, but Grandma and Mama were right. She was expecting, her courses already two weeks late. One night. She would hate for Duncan to never know about their child, would never keep the knowledge from him as the knowledge of his true birth mother had been kept from him. He was to be a father, and she needed to tell him. With a nod, she murmured, "I want to go."

"Then we'll attire ourselves correctly and leave within the hour." With one hand raised high, Grandma signaled Ethan and Grandpa as they both practiced with the bow and arrow across the other side of the meadow. "We leave for Ardan."

Ethan and Grandpa strode across and Ethan extended his hand to her and tugged her to her feet. "We'll be with you every step of the way."

"Aye, as you always have been." She hugged him and trekked inside.

In her chamber which she'd shared with Mama this past month, she changed into her darkest clothing to hide her form as best as she could for their trip out on the water. Black breeches donned, she tucked the hem of her black tunic in then bundled her hair under an equally dark woolen cap. With her black cloak on and Mama and Grandma wearing similar dark attire, she walked outside and joined Grandpa and Ethan as the sun lowered on the horizon.

"Are we all ready?" Ethan slung a satchel over his shoulder.

"Aye, as ready as we'll ever be." Mama hooked one arm through both hers and Grandma's and they walked together along the tree-lined trail toward Kinloch harbor.

As the dark fully descended and the moon rose, only a slight curve of golden yellow in the night sky, they cleared the woods and arrived at the entrance to Kyle Rhea. Breathing deep of the fresh sea air, she hopped on board her grandparents' skiff secured to its mooring. Ethan raised the sail while Grandpa sat at the stern and gripped the rudder. The wind blew and the pine trees rising high on her left swayed, while across the thin kyle on her right, the mainland rose. Ardan House beckoned.

* * * *

Slouched in the padded armchair in his chamber, Duncan took a long swig of the ale from his tankard, the drink doing naught to dull his endless pain. Legs stretched out and crossed at the ankle before the fire, the night sky beyond his window haunted him. With the passing of each day this past month, he'd joined his men as they sailed alongside the length and breadth of his land in their attempt to halt the MacDonald in his raids and attacks, their last battle a deadly one fought right here on Loch Carron. Now though, with the MacDonald retreating back to Skye, he sorely hoped for a small reprieve from the warring.

"My laird." A knock rattled his door. "'Tis Ivor. You have a visitor, well actually you have five visitors, but only one wishes to speak with you right this very moment."

"I've no wish to greet new arrivals this night, but by all means ensure they have a pallet to sleep on in the great hall and I'll talk to them in the morn." Behind him, his door swung open and he growled under his breath then shoved to his feet. "I said—"

Ivor didn't stand there, only a hallucination of his wife.

"Ella?" He dropped his tankard and it crashed to the floor, ale splashing the hearth and flames and making the fire sizzle. Thoughts of this woman had plagued him every waking hour since he'd left her, and now she appeared exactly as he'd envisioned her, dressed in lad's clothing, her cheeks and nose pink and her hair bundled up under a black woolen cap. She was his every dream come true.

"Aye, 'tis me, and you look terrible." She pulled thick fur gloves off her hands and stuffed them into the pocket of her black cloak.

"Are you really here?"

"I am." She searched his gaze, the gold flecks at the edge of her brown eyes flickering in the firelight.

"You shouldnae be here. Danger lurks if you're seen with me." He had to send her right back out and away.

"Mama and Ethan came with me, Grandpa and Grandma too, all disguised. We sailed from Skye, will leave while 'tis still dark as well, but I needed to speak to you this night and it cannae wait."

"Then speak, and make it quick."

"I still hate you." Her bottom lip wobbled. "So much it hurts."

"I still love you, so much it hurts." He shoved his hands behind his back to keep from reaching for her. "Was there aught else you wished to say?"

"Aye, I love you too."

"I know." He moved not an inch, even though all he wanted to do was sweep her up in his arms and toss her onto his four-poster bed so close behind her.

"Ivor informed me that you've successfully chased the MacDonald back to Dunscaith. That is news I had no' heard."

"For now, although I dinnae doubt he will return again afore too long."

"He isnae one to forgive and forget easily." She pulled the cap from her head and her long brown tresses cascaded down to her waist, the odd golden strand shimmering within the silky mass. Swaying a touch, she shrugged out of her cloak and laid it over the back of his armchair. "'Tis warm in here."

"You're making yourself rather at home in my chamber. If

you've said all you need to, then I want you to leave." Sending her away before he lost his resolve not to, hammered at him. Aye, maintaining her safety and protection was all that mattered and having her here at Ardan House wasn't acceptable. She'd surely placed her life in danger simply by coming here. Now, he needed to send her away, immediately.

"There is more I need to say." She closed her eyes then opened them again, wobbled and leaned against the back of his armchair. "I'm sorry. I've eaten little this day and what I do consume does no' always stay put."

"Then sit for a moment." He aided her to his bed and she eased down on the edge while he paced before her. "I can send for a tray if you like."

"Nay, I'll eat with my kin at the tavern. Mama longs to visit Mary and William and we shall do so afore returning to Skye."

"The MacDonald must never know you've set foot on my land. You must take care while at the tavern as well." He halted before her, lowered to his knees and swept a lock of her silky brown hair back from her face. Hell, he longed to touch more of her.

"The MacDonald is far away right now." Such need flared within her gaze, likely the same need that flared within his. "I've missed you, more than my heart can stand. Have you been well?"

"As well as can be."

"You've no' taken any injuries during your battles with the MacDonald?" She cupped his cheeks, stroked her fingers slowly back and forth along his jaw.

"Only the odd nick." He covered her hands with his, reveled in the sensation of her soft touch. "Dinnae forget that I hold the battle skill, Ella. That gives me far more strength than one man usually holds."

"I've seen that strength and skill for myself." She leaned closer, pressed her forehead to his, her mouth a mere breath away. "Would you kiss me?"

"That is one tempting offer, but one I'll have to decline."

"Please, just one kiss." She licked his lower lip and he released a low rumble.

"Damn it, woman."

"Kiss me." Her sweetly hypnotic voice swirled around him. "One more time."

Unable to deny her command, he seized her lips and molded their mouths together. She tasted like pure heaven, achingly beautiful and his restraint broke. He deepened their kiss, everything within him demanding the return of his mate and the only woman who'd ever hold the other half of his soul. Locking their bodies tighter together, he devoured her, tasting deeper and deeper until her soft little moans had him sweeping her black tunic over her head. He growled as her full breasts spilled forth, the tips beaded with stiff nipples he wanted to suck on.

"Aye, this is what I need. Make love to me, Duncan." Another compelling command, and he had no ability to fight it.

He hauled off her knee-high leather boots, almost tore her breeches in his eagerness to get to her and once her body was bared, his mouth watered and every rational thought fled his mind.

Her eyelids were half-lowered, her breath coming harder and faster, the same as his.

Gently, he glided his hands over her sides and under her lush bottom. "You take my breath away, Ella."

"I want more. Take your clothes off." A command of the deepest sort.

"Damn it, we're going to regret this. You need to cease compelling me." He pulled his boots off, shoved his black pants down his legs then stripped his shirt over his head. "Tell me to stop."

"Lie down." Another command.

"You arenae listening to me, woman."

"Right beside me."

He did as she bid and she crawled over top of him and sat astride his hips. Leaning forward, she brushed her breasts against his chest, pressed her lips to his neck and rubbed her entire body against his. His cock throbbed hot and hard between them.

"I will never regret any joining with you." She wrapped her fingers around his fiercely erect shaft.

Hell, he needed her, so badly, to have their bodies joined together and—sweet heaven. She grasped his shaft tighter and it pulsed in her fisted grip. So close. He was on the brink of coming right here and now, could barely hold onto his great need to join with her.

"You need me the same way I need you." She feasted her gaze on his straining member then bent and licked him with one hearty swipe right across the head. "I'm going to take you in my mouth."

A sizzling pressure buzzed at the base of his spine and his cock lengthened to the point of pain. Just the thought of her wrapping her lips around him made him so hard. Damn it. He'd never get through this moment if he didn't take back the control. "I want my wife," he muttered, teeth clenched.

"I'm no longer your wife, but you can take me all the same."

Aye, he'd steal this moment for them both and treasure it until the end of his days. He flipped her over and she squealed as she landed on her belly and bounced.

"Duncan." Smiling, she lifted up onto her hands and knees and wriggled her backside at him. "Is this how you want me?"

"Aye, so stay still." On his knees, he crawled in over top of her, eased one arm around her waist, her back heating his chest so deliciously. "Very still."

"Mmm, this position is interesting, and making me rather wet." She wriggled her pert backside at him, her silky brown hair sliding off her back and brushing his pillow as she peeked over her shoulder at him. "There are so many ways we've never loved each other."

"I need you, badly." He ran one hand underneath her raised body, over her swaying breasts and along the flat line of her belly, his need for her an unstoppable beat in his blood. Head dipped, he kissed her neck, nipped her ear then pushed his cock through her drenched folds and surged deep inside her. Perfect, so perfect, every single exquisite inch of her. He pumped in and out and his mind went dark with lust.

"More, give me more." She reached underneath her, cupped his balls slapping against her bottom and pushed her backside even deeper into his groin.

"You're my mate, my lover." He trailed one hand over her curls below, touched her nub and as she arched her back and cried out, he caressed the spot which always brought her such pleasure. Stroking her, he slammed balls-deep inside her, over and over again.

"Aye, always yours." She cried out as she shattered, her channel locking tight around his cock and making him lose all control.

He pushed all the way to her core and as her inner muscles clenched so deliciously around him, her body bathing him in a liquid heat he completely adored, he came, his seed shooting from him and coating her deep within.

"I love you, Duncan." She went limp in his arms.

"There is none I love more than you." Gently, he lowered her onto her front then pulled himself out of her. All he wanted to do was remain deep inside her, but the need to ensure her continued safety roared through him far stronger. He nabbed his pants and yanked them on. "Are you well? I didnae hurt you when I took you?"

"I'm feeling very well taken. You have my thanks." Sated, she rolled over onto her back and stretched.

"Then 'tis time for you to go." He jiggled her breeches up her legs, pulled her tunic over her head, laced her boots and grabbed her cloak and held it out to her. "Now, and never return. Do we have an understanding?"

* * * *

"Aye, we have an understanding." Mayhap she shouldn't have come to Ardan House after all, but she'd never regret this moment, of taking back her words of anger and ensuring he knew her true feelings. Heart still breaking, she swung her cloak over her shoulders and walked out his door, traversed the long length of the gloomy passageway and halted at the top of the stairwell. Aye, their situation was no different to how it had been when he'd last left her on Skye, except for one glaring issue. She now carried his child and—oh drat. She'd clear forgotten to tell him.

She turned around and lost her breath. He stood outside his door, his leather pants hanging loosely on his hips, his feet and chest bare and his blue eyes blazing with need.

"Go!" He stormed back inside his chamber and slammed his door shut. The harsh sound bounced off the stone walls, the wind rippling over the single candle burning in an iron wall sconce beside her.

The flame died out and she sank back into the darkened niche across from the stairs, tears flowing freely down her cheeks. Embracing the dark, she took a few necessary moments to breathe deep and clear her thoughts. Mayhap she'd tell Ivor about the babe instead. He could pass the message along to Duncan for her. As long as Duncan knew of the child, it mattered little who he learnt the truth from.

"Ella!" Duncan's door crashed open and he raced past her hidden spot, a mere blur as he bounded down the stairs still yelling her name.

Never could she give him up the way he'd given her up. She wiped her tears away with the collar of her cloak, his shouts continuing to echo, although they now seemed to be coming closer. Clearly he wished to make certain she was gone.

"Ella!" Footsteps pounded up the stairs and she stepped out of the niche as he made the top step. Half bent over, hands grasping his knees, he lugged in a deep breath. "Ivor said you hadn't left yet."

"I'm on my way. There's no need to tell me to leave yet again."

"I'm sorry." He straightened, raked one hand through his messy black locks and tumbled them about even more. "I shouldnae have spoken so harshly to you, have never done so with another woman afore, and I've certainly no desire to start now."

"I should be the one apologizing. I arrived unexpectedly, and you did expressly forbid me to come." She shoved her hands behind her back, wrung her fingers together. "You likely dinnae wish to hear this either, but I did come for a reason. If 'tis a boy I carry, I shall name him Hacon after my papa, and if a girl, Beth after your mother."

"Pardon?"

"There is to be a child born from our time together while handfasted."

"You're expecting?" His face paled.

"I am, and should you wish to see the child once born, then send a messenger to my village with the place and time you wish to meet. I will never deny you the time you need with our child. We will come, unless of course you wish only to see the child then Ethan can travel in my stead. Whatever you desire can be arranged."

"You're truly expecting?" His shock dispersed and sheer wonder coursed across his face. He caught her arms, pressed her back against the wall, his gaze roaming down her body to her belly. Gently, he spread his hand over her stomach and went completely still. "Truly?"

"Aye, I'm certain, although it took both Mama and Grandma to make me see the truth."

"My mother passed away during labor." Pained words and they made her heart ache with the desperate need he laced within them. "I cannae lose you that way."

"I would never allow death to take me, no' from you or our child, no matter we've parted ways." She looked into his eyes, wanting only to kiss him, for him to say he wanted her just as badly as she wanted him. "I could even compel myself to remain alive if need be."

"You can do that?" He kissed the tip of her nose then both cheeks before trailing down and nibbling on her lips.

"It cannae hurt to try," she mumbled between his kisses.

"Your belly with grow large with our child and I'll miss every moment of it." Still kissing her lips, he slid his hand under the hem of her tunic and softly caressed her skin. "I've already missed the first precious month. Have you been ill? When you arrived, you said you'd eaten little this day, and what you do consume does no' always stay put."

"Aye, but in truth, my desire for food has been gone since the day you left. Being parted as we have been hurts terribly, until I cannae see a way past the pain anymore. I miss being your wife, to the depths of my soul." Speaking the truth eased a little of her heartache, and having him this close, even more so. "Why are we allowing the MacDonald to control our actions, as well as the direction of our future?"

"To ensure the safety of your kin. Your grandparents live on Skye, right within his reach. Should he discover that we spoke handfast vows, he'll come after them, as well as Ethan and your mama. His need to retaliate right now is too strong." He slowly lowered to his knees, pushed her tunic up higher and rubbed his cheek against the bare skin of her belly.

"What if we all lived together, right here?" She'd be uprooting her kin, every single one of them, tearing her grandparents from their home on Skye and Mama and Ethan from their beloved village. Although keeping her child and its father apart was a thought she could barely tolerate.

"I cannae ask that of you and your kin."

"I believe I was the one doing the asking."

"They'd be forced to give up all they love and adore, their home and their clan." He shoved to his feet, hope burning bright in his eyes. "Although I'd offer them Ardan House as their own, my clan here as theirs. If I asked them to stay, would they agree? There is now a child to consider."

"We'll all be safe here, correct?"

"Aye, I'd ensure it." He searched her gaze. "If they agree, then I'm going to send for a priest immediately. I will wed you proper, then lock you in my chamber until I've loved every single inch of you, in every single possible way."

"I will certainly never speak handfast vows with you again, no' since you broke your last vow. A proper marriage it would have to be." Her heart lifted with the possibility of remaining right here with him, of never having to leave this place or her chosen one, to have all her loved ones so very close as well. "We'll ask them together."

"We'll ask them now." He scooped her up in his arms and strode downstairs with her, his muscles tight and his body so very tense.

"Walk slower." She wanted to hold onto this moment forever, for in these few heartbeats of time she finally held hope as she hadn't in one very long month. Either her greatest desire would soon be granted, or completely stolen away from her.

He slowed his step then halted in the great hall with its vaulted ceiling and high wooden beamed rafters rising to an imposing height. A sliver of moonlight shone through the tall windows and sprinkled across the wooden floorboards. Beside the blazing fireplace, two dogs snoozed and Duncan trod with her held close to his chest as he weaved around the perimeter of the hall filled with dozens of trestle tables.

Her heart expanded, barely containing the love she held for him within it. "Kiss me." One fiercely whispered command. "I want to be your wife."

"I want to be your husband, to raise our child right here at Ardan." He slowed, captured her mouth with his and kissed her, with a passion that made her head spin and made her wish they could return to his chamber and bolt the door.

When he broke their kiss, she wanted to demand he kiss her all over again but her kin awaited them at the dais. All were seated and partaking of a late evening meal, platters of breads, meats and cheeses gracing the center of the long table, a dish of pastries and small cakes too.

Mama waved her over. "Come, sit and eat. I've just met Hamish and he's spoken of some most interesting things he's just *seen* within a vision."

"As in?" Duncan asked as he carried her to the high platform and pulled out a chair. He eased down into it and settled her on his lap, bound his arms tightly around her waist.

"Mayhap Hamish should elaborate." Mama grinned at the fae seer.

Eyeing Duncan, Hamish popped an apple pastry in his mouth and chewed. "I informed Ella's kin of what I saw unfold while the two of you spoke just now, and of course of the bairns I saw Ella carrying. Provided they agree to remain here, in just under eight months Ella will give birth to a son named Hacon and a wee daughter named Beth. They will be your first and second-born, twins just as you and Coll are, and both gifted in the way of the fae."

"I'm carrying twins?" Shock and immense joy collided within her.

"Aye, my sweet." Mama hugged her, her smile wide. "And provided we all agree to remain at Ardan, then all will be well."

Duncan cleared his throat then cast his gaze from Mama to

her grandparents then Ethan. "Then I would ask something most important of you all, right this moment. If you choose to live here, I'll ensure your protection, as well as give you my undying gratitude. Be my kin, just as I wish to be yours."

Smiling, Grandpa lifted his tankard and took a hearty swig of ale. "We've already made ourselves at home, Duncan, and we have no need to return to Skye where the MacDonald can rule over us. Here, he can hold no control, so aye, we accept your offer, all of us."

"I'm asking a great deal." Duncan tightened his hold on her. "There's a war raging and I've no idea when it will ever end. If you need more time to consider my request, you have it."

"The war rages no matter where we live." Ethan rose and extended his hand to Duncan. "You have my agreement in remaining too, provided you allow me to train amongst your men and they can accept my presence."

"Without question. I look forward to training with you too."

"I accept your offer as well." Mama hugged Duncan, her giddiness shining through. "There is no other place for me, other than right here with my most beloved kin."

"And I go wherever my loved ones go." Grandma clapped and beamed. "Although we must return home for long enough to collect our animals and belongings."

"I cannae believe you've all said aye." Pure joy lit Duncan's face.

"They've truly agreed." Joy infused her as well and kissing her mate, her heart overflowed with love. "I didnae even need to compel them either," she whispered against his lips, "and I was fully prepared to do so in case you're wondering."

"I'd hoped you would should the need arise." He grinned and she clung to him.

Aye, this day marked the beginning of the rest of their lives together, and a most wondrous life she intended for it to be. Giggling, she kissed her chosen one again and tasted sheer

pleasure and all the delights it could bring.
Never would she live apart from him again.
He was her life, her love, the other half of her very soul.

Chapter 12

Cloaked and unseen at the far end of the great hall of Ardan House, Cherub snagged Kirk's hand and drew him outside into the stony courtyard. A sliver of moonlight shimmered through the wispy cloud drifting over it while the air swirled and whispered across her skin, bringing to her all the secrets it held.

"What do you sense now, my elusive imp?" Kirk wrapped her up in his arms and smothered her in his delicious and heady scent.

"This is what I live for, to see each mated pair join together as one. I'm so excited for Ella and her kin, that Duncan has asked them to remain here. This is where they all belong, and what I sense now is that a new clan MacKenzie rises, one beyond the devious and dominating hand of Colin MacKenzie."

"As do I. Where are we off to next?"

"'Tis time for us to track down Coll as he searches MacKenzie land in his quest to gather more warriors to his and Duncan's cause. He needs to come home, where he might finally be reunited with his chosen one."

"Reunited?" Kirk frowned and she grinned.

"Aye. It appears Coll and his mate have ignored the call within their fae blood to accept each other, but no more will I allow that. We'll guide Coll in the right direction now his chosen one is no longer beyond his reach."

This coming chase for Coll would be one of the most intriguing she'd ever set in motion, a journey of discovery for two soul bound mates who no longer had to deny either each other or their bond.

"Then lead the way." Kirk twirled her around, captured her mouth with his and kissed her, his passion flaring hot and strong, the same as hers always did for him. None could ever deny the mated bond, and she'd certainly ensure each mated pair amongst her people had the chance to find each other.

With a giggle against Kirk's lips, she sent them both soaring high into the skies and amongst the brilliance of the radiant stars above. This was life, to have the one who held the other half of their soul always at their side.

With her own heart and soul soaring at the incredible beauty surrounding her, she gave into her need to join with her chosen one, right within the vivid heights of the night sky.

Love. It was now Duncan and Ella's too, would hopefully soon come for Coll and his mate. Aye, so many adventures still awaited them all.

Author's Note

In the twelfth century, clan Matheson settled around the area of Loch Alsh, Loch Carron, and Kintail, and gave their allegiance to clan MacDonald whose chiefs were the Lords of the Isles. Clan Matheson became a large and powerful clan with a force of around two-thousand men, although by the middle of the sixteenth century they'd diminished greatly in size and influence due to the blood feuds raging across the isles at that time. This warring left them to possess less than a third of their original Matheson property on Loch Alsh.

It's also well known in history that clan Matheson also forged an alliance with clan MacKenzie during the middle ages, which meant at times the two clans fought side by side, yet also against each other when clan Matheson found themselves stuck in the middle of the feuding between the MacDonalds and the MacKenzies. Within this series my hope is to capture the difficulties faced between these two great clans, and all while spinning stories in my own unique way.

Certainly across all the books I've written involving the three clans of Matheson, MacKenzie, and MacDonald, I've tried my best to show how their feuding and alliances made, moved back and forth throughout the years. I dearly love all these clans, can understand their struggles and losses, their conquests and wins, as well as how they attempted to remain as honorable as they could throughout it all.

In this story I've made mention of Dunscaith Castle, the stronghold of clan MacDonald on the Isle of Skye. Dunscaith Castle was first known as "Dun Sgathaich" and has strong ties to the heroes and heroines of Celtic legend. The castle itself is named after the legendary Scottish warrior woman Sgathaich, a great teacher of the martial arts, and arts of combat. Dunscaith Castle sits at the mouth of Loch Eishort and dates back to the early 1300s, although a castle or fortification of some type has in fact occupied this site from a far earlier date. For the purposes of this story, I've kept that earlier dated stronghold's name as Dunscaith Castle to better describe the location's setting for clan MacDonald in this era of the 1200s I've written within.

This story is woven with as much accuracy to the period and locations as possible, although any mistakes made are mine alone. Please feel free to search for any of my other works. I simply adore strong heroines, and have a ton of fun matching them with their honorable alpha heroes.

**Also available in paperback
Scottish Historical Romance**

Traveling through time…for a Highlander.

Highlander Heat Series

Highlander's Castle, Book One

Highlander's Magic, Book Two

Highlander's Charm, Book Three

Highlander's Guardian, Book Four

Highlander's Faerie, Book Five

Highlander's Champion, Book Six

by Joanne Wadsworth

Looking for more sexy Scottish adventure?

Catch a teaser excerpt of the next book in this series.

Highlander's Touch

The Matheson Brothers, Book Nine

by Joanne Wadsworth

Highlander's Touch

The Matheson Brothers, Book Nine

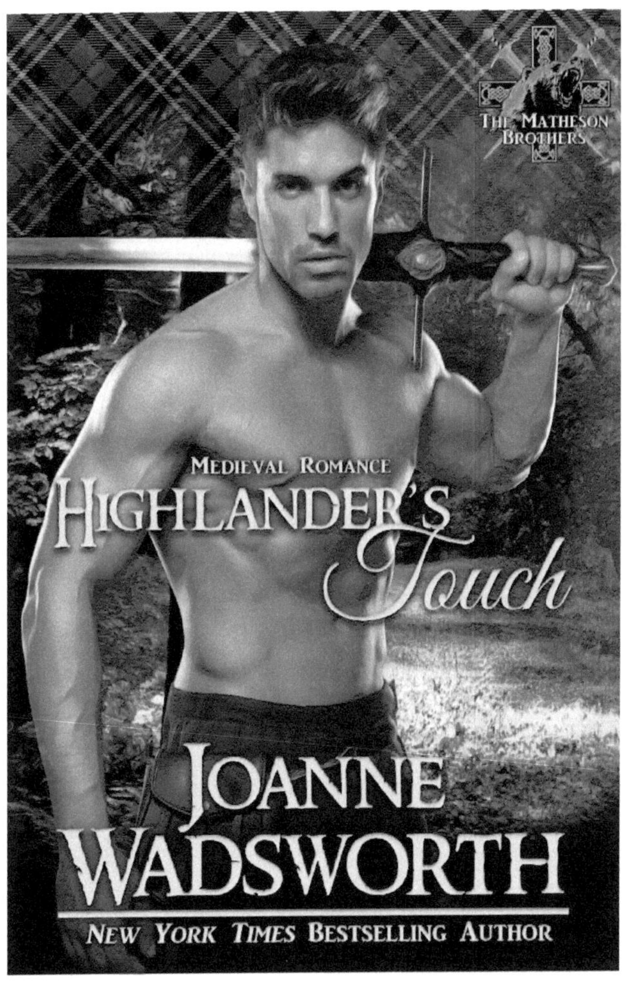

Teaser Excerpt

Fiona had never seen Coll so stripped down and very naked before.

Back a step, she inched until she hit her back on the corner bedpost. She cast her gaze down his impressively built body once more, his muscles all sleek and hard and—she cleared her throat. "So, I see you're a big man, ah, everywhere."

"Aye, I'm most definitely dreaming, because that is exactly what I would have wanted you to say when you first looked upon me." The gold flecks flickered brighter in his stunning brown eyes and with one finger crooked, he motioned for her to come back to him. "Dinnae be afraid of me, my fiery empath."

"I've never been afraid of you, but then I've never quite seen you like this afore." Return she would though. She inched forward, until the tips of her toes touched the tips of his bare toes, then she tipped her chin up and looked him in the eyes. "You appeared to be enjoying your bath, while you spoke my name."

"Aye, I always do speak of you when I bathe and dream like this." He wrapped his hands around her waist, dipped her back off her feet and touched his mouth to hers. He kissed her, so whisper-soft, as if he wished to savor the taste of her then with a low growl, he deepened their kiss, his tongue sliding over hers in a kiss that completely scattered all her thoughts.

Naught had ever felt so right.

Coll was kissing her, for the first time, and he was completely naked too.

The Matheson Brothers Continued

Highlander's Kiss, Book Four
Highlander's Heart, Book Five
Highlander's Sword, Book Six

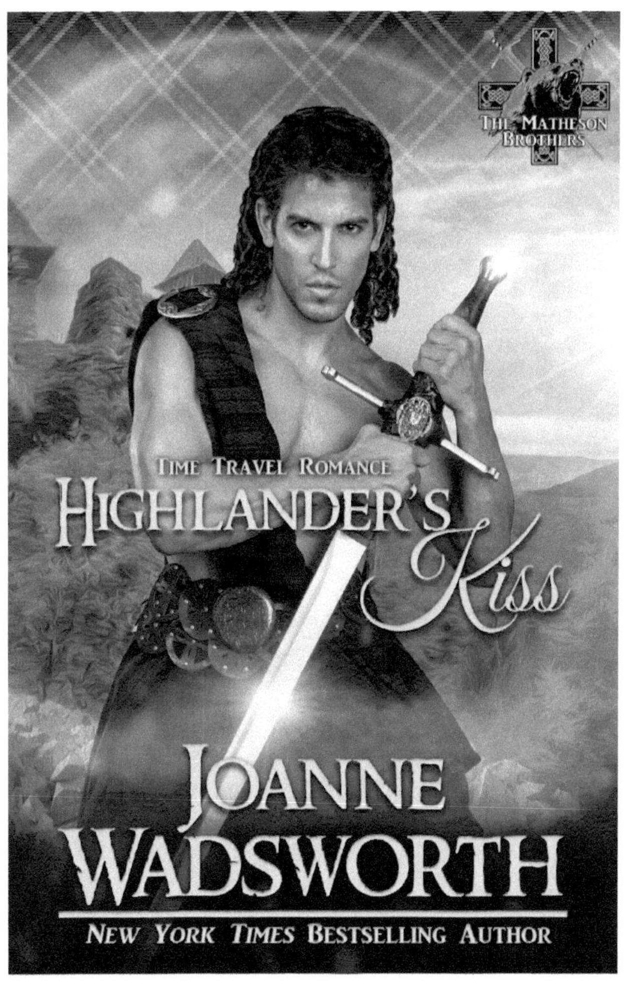

JOANNE WADSWORTH

The Matheson Brothers Continued

Highlander's Bride, Book Seven
Highlander's Caress, Book Eight
Highlander's Touch, Book Nine

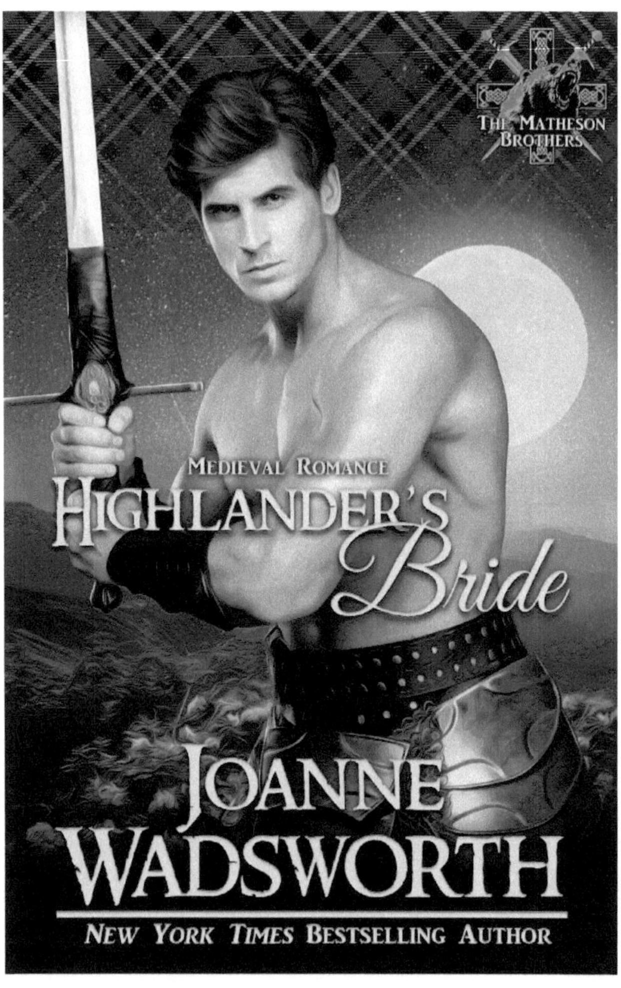

The Matheson Brothers Continued

Highlander's Shifter, Book Ten
Highlander's Claim, Book Eleven
Highlander's Courage, Book Twelve
Highlander's Mermaid, Book Thirteen

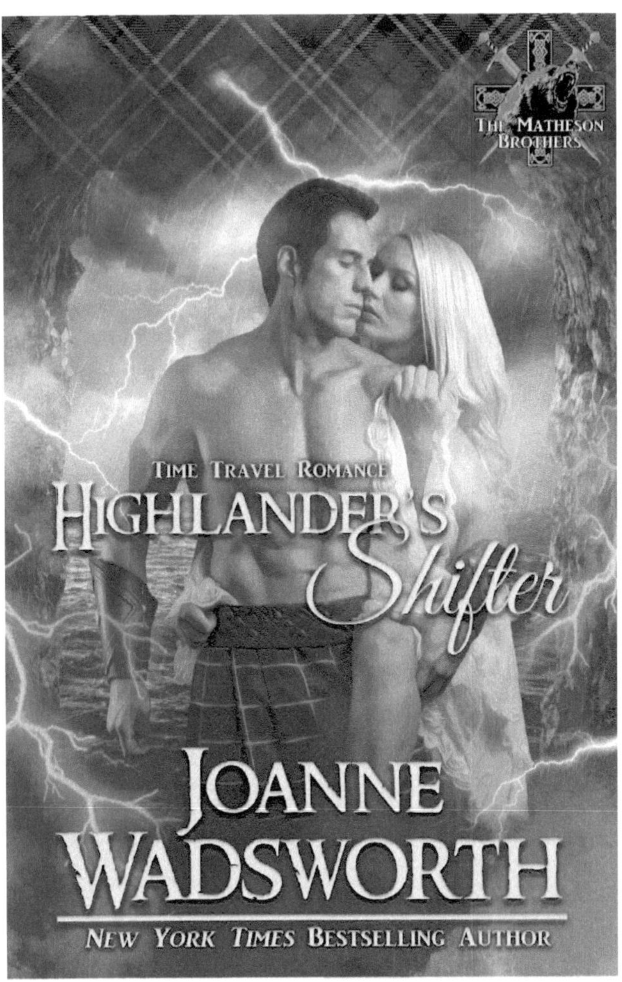

Regency Brides

The Duke's Bride, Book One
The Earl's Bride, Book Two
The Wartime Bride, Book Three
The Earl's Secret Bride, Book Four
The Prince's Bride, Book Five
Her Pirate Prince, Book Six

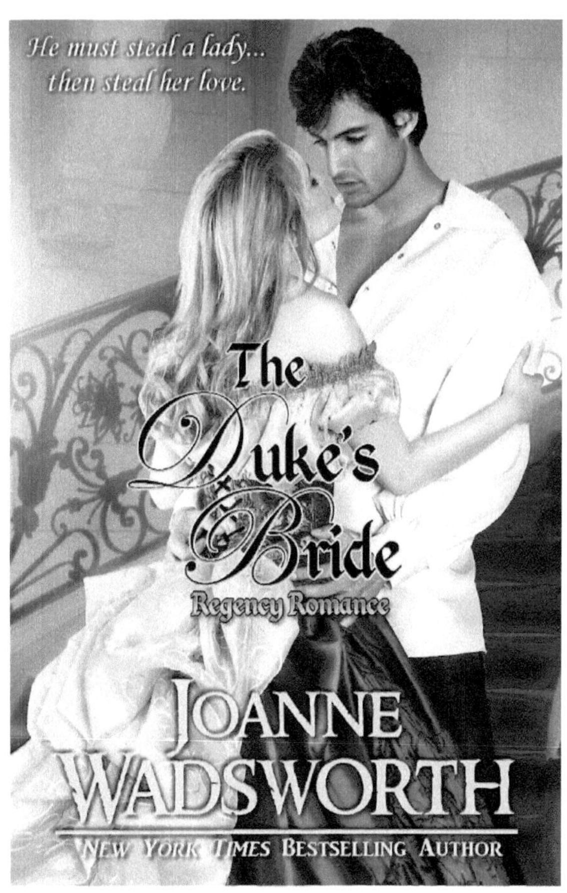

Billionaire Bodyguards

Billionaire Bodyguard Attraction, Book One
Billionaire Bodyguard Boss, Book Two
Billionaire Bodyguard Fling, Book Three

JOANNE WADSWORTH

Joanne Wadsworth is a *New York Times* and *USA Today* Bestselling Author who adores getting lost in the world of romance, no matter what era in time that might be. Hot alpha Highlanders hound her, demanding their stories are told and she's devoted to ensuring they meet their match, whether that be with a feisty lass from the present or far in the past.

Living on a tiny island at the bottom of the world, she calls New Zealand home. Big-dreamer, hoarder of chocolate, and addicted to juicy watermelons since the age of five, she chases after her four energetic children and has her own hunky hubby on the side.

So come and join in all the fun, because this kiwi girl promises to give you her "Hot-Highlander" oath, to bring you a heart-pounding, sexy adventure from the moment you turn the first page. This is where romance meets fantasy and adventure…

To learn more about Joanne and her works, visit
http://www.joannewadsworth.com